I0788575

Escape

Book One - Eight Realm Series

Entertainment Enterprise
Harker Heights, Texas 76548
Entertainmententerprise.net

Frist Edition December 2020

The publisher is not responsible for websites (or their content) that are not owned by the publisher.

ISBN 978-1-947040-00-7

Printed in the United States of America

Escape

Book One - Eight Realm Series

Catherine Sitz

Chapter One

The Beginning

Seventeen-year-old Sierra Winslow brushed her long straight brown hair out of her eyes. She scanned the titles of the hard-back books that were crammed into every inch of the metal shelves, packed into all the available space of the crowded bookstore. Tracing the worn bindings with the tip of her red polished fingernail, she pulled a smooth, dark leather book off the shelf and caressed the cover before tucking it beneath her arm.

Quickly making her way through the maze of used books stacked to the ceiling, she managed to wind her way back to the front of the used book store. The sunlight streamed through the floor to ceiling windows illuminating the dust mites floating in the air. She smiled to herself. The place was magical.

She laid the leather book on the smooth glass counter and smiled at the white-haired woman behind it.

Mabel Lewis picked up the book and raised one perfectly drawn on eyebrow and smiled. "Odd choice for a young lady," she declared.

Sierra shrugged. "It's for a school project."

Mabel rang up the purchase and put the book in a pink plastic bag with a stack of books embossed on the glossy surface. "Good luck with your project."

Sierra handed her the money and picked up the bag. "Thank you. I need all of the luck I can get," she said smiling.

Sierra pulled her four-year-old gray Honda up to the curb, grabbed her purse and the bag off the gray leather seat and climbed out of the car, just as her best friend, Bree drove up in her red sports car. Bree's short blond hair was pulled away from her face, showing off her big green eyes.

'Hey," Bree said. "A bunch of us are going swimming over at Tim's. Want to come?"

Sierra frowned. "I can't. I have to work on my stupid project, and I haven't even started."

"That sucks." Bree said. "Would you turn your phone up, so the next time I don't have to drive all the way over here to ask you?"

"Sorry. I forgot to turn it up after I left the bookstore."

"Are you sure you can't come for a little while?" she pleaded teasingly.

"I wish. It's due the day after tomorrow and I have to get a good grade or I'm beyond grounded."

'Okay. I'll stop by later and see if you need some help."

Sierra laughed. "Okay. Have fun. Tell everyone hi for me."

Bree waved and drove away.

Sierra's silky white cat, Fluffy raced up the carpeted stairs in front of her and curled up on the edge of Sierra's queen size bed, watching her intently.

She pulled the book out of the pink bag and the cat stuck her head inside investigating it. Sierra laid across the teal green comforter on her stomach and started reading. Fluffy pawed at the bag, purring.

The book doesn't hold her interest so she flipped through the pages absently until she reached the end, groaning. Frowning slightly, she tried to make out a poem written in very small elegant writing in the back of the book.

Squinting, she held the book closer so she could read the tiny print.

Our world collides.

Shifting and changing.

We must survive.

Forever engaging.

Souls entwined.

Spirits unrest.

Returning at our bequest.

Sierra read it silently and frowned. It didn't rhyme or make any sense. Maybe if she read it aloud it would sound better.

Our world collides.

Shifting and changing.

Fluffy raised her head and mewed softly.

We must survive.

Forever engaging.

The cat stretched and watched Sierra intently.

Souls entwined.

Spirits unrest.

Fluffy grew agitated. She pawed at the book in Sierra's hand.

Returning at our bequest.

A cool wind whipped through her bedroom, ruffling the posters on her wall and scattered the contents of her messy dresser across the room, slamming the book shut. Sierra jumped back, startled.

Fluffy shook herself and glared at Sierra intently.

She stared around the room in confusion. "Where in the hell did that wind come from?"

"How should I know?" answered Fluffy.

Sierra's eyes widened in shock as she stared at the cat, then laughed and relaxed. "Okay, Adam. Very funny. You can come out now."

"Your brother went to the mall with your mother," Fluffy stated matter-of-factly, licking her paw absently.

Sierra blinked twice. Her eyes were wide with shock. She kept them on Fluffy as she slowly rose from the bed, and backed away.

She raced to the door, threw it open and ran down the stairs, taking them two at a time.

Fluffy jumped off the bed, following right behind her.

"You need to get a grip," she said to herself as she paused to unlock the solid wood front door. Pushing down the panic that threatened to engulf her and turned around to face the cat.

If a cat could smile, Fluffy was smiling. "Yes, I'm really talking, and we need to have a talk. You had better sit down first."

Sierra slowly sat down on the bottom step, staring at the fluffy white cat, her mind struggling to come to terms with a talking cat.

Chapter Two

Mags

"I apologize for frightening you. Let me introduce myself. My name is Mags. You just read a releasing spell, which is why I am able to talk." The cat shook her head trying to clear her thoughts. "Where was I? You broke the spell that rendered me speechless."

"How?" Sierra asked stunned. This wasn't possible.

"Oh dear, how long have we been here? I have to return...."

The crystal blue palace sparkled and glittered in the moonlight. The silver blue spires reached toward the stars, casting a rainbow of light across the courtyard below.

Seated on a throne decorated with stars and moonbeams sat the queen of the Eight Realms. She wore a silver blue dress that matched the sky and stars above. Her long white hair was woven through with tiny stars that shimmered when she moved.

A crystal-clear river wound its way through the court. Rainbow fish leaped out of the water, releasing thousands of bubbles that float gently through the air.

The crowd of well-dressed ladies, gentlemen and animals oohed and awed in delight.

Tiny butterflies flitted between the bubbles. Their wings lit up for tonight's celebration. Their tiny red lips smiled broadly as they flew through the crowd.

The Queen raised her hands, and the ceiling above the guest transformed into the night sky.

The crowd roared in delight. A dark shadowy cloud weaved in and out of the guest making its way through the crowd, then taking the form of a young man in front of the Queen. His clothes were dark and flowed around his tall slender form.

The young Queen smiled. "Welcome Lord Dak. What a pleasant surprise."

"Not so pleasant my Lady," he replied licking his sharp pointed teeth.

The Queen hid her surprise. Her thoughts were churning away at the reason for Dak's rude intrusion. Her eyes scanned the crowd. She saw Kindrick, one of her soldiers, blond head above the crowd. He was purposefully making his way toward her, while Slate and Rhys closed in on Dak.

"My people are tired of being excluded from your celebrations," Dak growled roughly.

"My Lord, your people were invited, but due to your dislike of everything bright, you declined."

"That's why it's time for a change. Darkness is about to fall on the other seven realms."

A look of horror was written on every face in the crowd. The Queen's gaze scanned the crowd filled with her frightened people. Her gaze returned to Dak. Fury flashed in her dark blue eyes, but she remained quiet.

"We will no longer have to sneak through the night. There will be eternal darkness."

Slade and Rhys flanked each side of Dak.

Wisps of dark shadows circled the celebration extinguishing the lights. The butterflies' lights blinked and went out. They cried out in fear and raced toward the Queen.

Twelve dark forms took shape around the celebration, surrounding the crowd.

The Queen smiled sadly. "Dak, our people have lived in peace for generations. Think long and hard before you do this," she warned.

Dak's deep dark laugh filled the air. "I've done nothing else, my Lady."

The Queen frowned. "Very well."

She raised her pale slender hands. Four white tornados appeared. In a blink of an eye, they swirled, moving throughout the crowd, gathering up the guests, carrying them through the glittering gates that acted as doorways to the other realms, and safely home.

Dak growled in anger. His form dissolved into a shadow, and he raced toward the Queen.

She raised her palms to the ceiling and the stars burst into light.

Dak took form and crashed to the ground. His skin was smoldering. He quickly rolled beneath the shade of a tapestry. His followers did the same.

A book floated in front of the Queen, using her finger, she quickly inscribed a spell on its pages. The book slammed shut and floated next to her.

Her voice, loud and musical filled the air. Her people waited expectantly for her to move them to safety. A white tornado formed enveloping everyone. "Alis veritas compori," she cried.

The outdoor room filled with a bright light, blinked, then plunged into darkness. "I will be back," the Queen warned.

Dak and his followers rose to their feet in the dark deserted room. An unnatural smile spread across his pale face. He brushed his long dark hair away from his eyes. "Nice of her to leave," he laughed. "Let's ready our army and find them. We have the other realms to take over."

They dissolved into their shadowy form and made their way through the deserted party, out into the cool night, toward the gate that led to their realm.

The silver gate shimmered and sparkled. The shadowy forms tried to pass through, but nothing happened. They raced to the other gate located on the other side of the realm and were unable to pass through.

They took their human form. "What has she done?" Dak cried. "She's separated the realms, trapping us here."

Every animal and insect imaginable appear out of nothing in the middle of a field. A loud splash echoed in the distance and an old book landed in the grass, left alone as the animals disappeared into the darkness.

Sierra's eyes were wide with disbelief. "That was you?"

"Yes, unfortunately I chose the wrong spell for a world with limited magic." Lady Mags wiped her eye with her paw. "I have no way of knowing how long we've been gone, but I have to get back. The moment you read the spell, the realms started moving back into place. I have to return before that happens."

Still struggling to process everything that Mags said, Sierra didn't want her to leave so soon.

Mags studied Sierra closely. "You should come with me. You shouldn't have been able to break the spell and I would like to discover how you did."

Sierra frowned in confusion. "I can't go with you. What about my family, school?"

"You have to possess magic to work magic. Don't you want to know what else you can do?"

Sierra slowly rose to her feet and paced back and forth across the glossy wooden floor. A world with magic. How could she pass up the opportunity to visit such a place?

And if Mags was right, and she did possess the ability to do magic, didn't she want to know? "If I go, I can't stay long. My parents will be furious."

"You will be entering a world like nothing you've ever seen before," Mags said.

Chapter Three

The Return

Mags followed Sierra back up the stairs to her bedroom. Sierra sat down on her bed, and Mags jumped up next to her.

Looking around at the normalcy of her room, the last few minutes seemed even more unreal.

Mags drew her back, saying, "Hold onto the book and take my paw. I need to draw on your strength," she instructed.

"Wait," said Sierra. She quickly raced around the room throwing clothes, toothbrush, toothpaste and other necessities into her backpack and slipped it over one shoulder. She clasped the book tightly in one hand and gently took Mags' white paw. "I'm ready."

"Are you certain this is what you want?"

"I'm sure."

Mags lifted her paw.

Sierra couldn't tell that anything was happening and suddenly felt very foolish.

A white tornado, invisible to most, traveled quickly and silently across the globe collecting Mags' people, then vanished. "*Alvis veritas compori resti*" Mags whispered.

Sierra felt a slight chill, blinked, and opened her eyes to a strange new world.

The Realm of Bresslewood was bathed in a dark mist, making it difficult to see. Sierra gripped the book tighter and looked down expecting to see Mags at her feet. Instead, she saw the hem of a silver blue dress. Her gaze jerked up into the blue eyes of a startling beautiful woman. Her long white hair had stars woven in its thick tresses.

"I don't understand," she stammered.

Mags smiled warmly. "I'm Lady Mags. The Queen of the Eight Realms."

"But… you're a cat?"

Mags laughed warmly. "Yes, I am. I can transform. We all can." She waved her arm toward the crowd behind them.

Sierra felt panic rising up in her chest. She clutched the book protectively in front of her. "I don't understand."

Mags linked her fingers with Sierra's. "Don't be afraid. We all possess the magic of transformation." Mags turned to her hundreds of subjects behind her. "Return to your animal form and stay out of sight until I can determine the threat we face."

Sierra watched in shock and surprise as the crowd transformed into dogs, cats, insects, frogs, fish, and animals she didn't recognize.

Mags squeezed her hand reassuringly. She turned to her soldiers lined up waiting for instructions. They nodded their heads in unison.

A decorative invitation appeared out of nothing and Mags handed it to one of her soldiers. "Hand deliver this to the leaders of these five realms. Then stand guard at each of the gates and allow no one through without the invitation. Please hurry. The gates will be open soon."

The guard turned and handed an invitation to the other guards and they raced off toward the shimmering gates, one on each side of the realm

Sierra looked over at Mags. "How?"

"Magic my dear. Magic is a major part of our lives. You will get used to it."

Sierra's eyes widened in disbelief. "I don't know about that."

A few minutes later, two colorful butterflies with human bodies flew in front of them. "The commander wanted you to know that our gates are secured."

"Thank you Fluris. Now hide in the forest until I know it is safe to return to the kingdom."

Fluris nodded her head and quickly disappeared into the darkness.

"She's beautiful." Sierra whispered softly.

"Yes, she is." Mags agreed. She turned to the remaining soldiers. "We need to get to the castle. It won't take Dak and his men long to figure out that the gates are open. We have to deal with him before anymore of his 'kind' try to get through."

"Yes, my Lady." Slade replied.

"We will enter the castle through the secret entrance and pray they haven't located it," Mags said. "Once we are inside I will rid the kingdom of this wretched darkness."

Mags raised her hands above her head and whispered softly to herself. A darker mist wrapped itself around them making all of them appear invisible. "Hurry, we don't have much time." Still holding tightly to Sierra's hand, she led the way through the forest, across a cobblestone bridge, their footsteps swallowed up by the mist.

They came to a stop next to a vine covered wall that seemed to appear out of nowhere. Mags gently touched the wall and it faded in front of them.

She didn't hesitate, and pulled Sierra through the opening behind her. Mags took note of the dirt covering the stairs. "We've been gone for a while," she said sadly.

She pushed against the wall and a door opened into a large room. Mags shook off the darkness surrounding them, crossed the room, waving her hand at the windows and doors. A darkness covered the windows and an invisible lock secured the door.

"If they detect us, they won't be able to get in," she explained for Sierra's benefit. Mags raised her hands toward the ceiling. The room grew brighter. She swept her hands across the room and the cobwebs and dirt vanished. Mags smiled and turned to Sierra. "I need you to read the spell. Pause, and read it again. I need to make certain that there are no remnants of the spell remaining. I need to be at my strongest to clear the darkness."

Sierra open the book, cleared her throat and read:

Our world collides.

Shifting and changing.

We must survive.

Forever engaging.

Souls entwined.

Spirits unrest.

Returning at our bequest.

A shimmering light surrounded Mags and lifted her off her feet. The light blinked and Sierra started again.

Our world collides.

Shifting and changing.

We must survive.

Forever engaging.

Souls entwined.

Spirits unrest.

Returning at our bequest.

The light grew brighter and brighter. Sierra shielded her eyes from its brilliance. The light exploded, clearing the remaining darkness from the room.

Mags dropped to her feet and staggered to maintain her balance.

"That was amazing," Sierra said astonished. "Are you okay?"

Mags crossed the room and quickly took Sierra's hands between hers. "I'm more than okay. That was amazing, but it wasn't me. It was you."

"That's impossible."

Mags pulled Sierra across the room and pulled her down next to her on the massive sofa covered in an ice blue leather. "I told you that you have magic in you, and you just proved it, and its strong magic."

Sierra stared at Mags in shock. How could she possibly possess magic? This was too much to take in.

Mags rose and quickly wrapped Slade, Rhys and their soldiers in a dark mist to conceal them. "Find Dak and his men and bring them to the castle." Dark cloaks appear across their arms. "Those will protect them when the darkness fades. Take them to the dungeon, and let me know when you have them."

"Yes, your majesty." Slade said, and is followed by Rhys and the soldiers, vanishing through the door, that disappeared behind them.

"Come, we have to hurry." Mags led Sierra up the back stairs to her bedroom. She raced to a marble table, waved her hand over the table and a crystal box appeared. She opened the box and pulled out a crystal bowl and three crystal vials with glowing liquid inside.

"Dak's magic is dark. So, I need to use strong light magic to dispel it after all this time."

"You still don't have any idea how long you've been gone?"

"No, but longer than I intended. I sent my people to your world to protect them. I didn't realize the spell was too strong for a world with limited magic. I am so grateful that you found the book and cast the spell to release us."

"Why were you in your animal form?"

"So we wouldn't raise alarms when we arrived in your world. My plan was to arrive, plan our next move and return home. For some reason in our animal form we quickly forgot who we were. We owe you our lives."

"I'm so glad I found your book."

"I can return you home whenever you'd like. I hope you will remain here so and I can help you discover your magic. But first, I need to break the darkness spell."

Mags pulled the crystal stopper out of the bottle filled with a glowing yellow liquid and poured one-third of it into the crystal bowl. A bright yellow light filled the room with its warmth.

She replaced the stopper and put the bottle back into the crystal box. The bottle quickly refilled itself.

Sierra raised one eyebrow with interest and wonder. This place was like nothing she could have imagined.

Mags smiled and winked at her. She repeated the process with the orange and red liquid. Each time the room was bathed in its warmth and color.

Mags gently stirred the colorful contents with her finger, mixing them together with a rainbow of color. The room filled with the rainbow, then it burst through the walls and windows, dissolving the dark mist Mags had shielded the windows with.

Sierra raced to the window. The rainbow streaked through the sky turning the darkness into daylight. The leaves on the trees turned from brown to green, red, blue and yellow. The water changed from a brown sludge to a vibrant blue.

The grass threw off its dry brown coat for one of blue green and flowers of every shade grew and bloomed across the kingdom.

Quaint homes turned from black to every shade of the rainbow.

Sierra gasped. "It's beautiful. Why on earth would anyone want to turn everything dark?"

Mags joined Sierra at the window and smiled, overjoyed to see her home return to how she left it. "Dak and his people are from a dark realm. They can't survive for long in this realm except at night. The night we came to your world, they threatened to take over this realm and in our absence, it stayed dark.

But while we were trapped on your world, they were trapped here. I'm sure they are both eager and angry at our return. They could either return home and forget their foolish threat, or pick up where they left off."

Chapter Four

Dak

Dak watched in surprise as four white tornadoes appeared out of nothing, divided and engulfed the members of the visiting four realms and whisked them away.

The darkened stars burst into light, forcing Dak to dive for the shadow of a tapestry draped across the room.

He hoped that his friends made it safely out of the murderous light. He watched in surprise as a book floated in front of the queen. His mind raced for a way to regain control of the situation.

Another tornado whipped through the crowd, engulfing everyone, leaving the queen, her people, Dak and his men. Dak couldn't hear her, but he could see her lips moving. To his astonishment, the lights blinked out, and he jumped to his feet and sprinted toward Mags.

She couldn't see him in the darkness, but he could clearly see her. He nearly reached her when her voice filled the dark room. "I'll be back," she said.

She vanished just as he reached out for her, his fingers closed on the cool air. He stood in front of her throne. A smile spread across his pale handsome face. Well played my lady, he thought to himself.

His men quickly joined him. "Nice of her to leave." He laughed.

"Let's ready our army and find them. We have other realms to take over."

They dissolved into wisps of dark shadows and flew across Bresslewood to the gate, the entrance to their home, the Dark Realm. The silver gate shimmered in the darkness. They tried to pass through, nothing happened. Their dark forms raced through the forest, back across Bresslewood, to the other gate with the same result. They couldn't pass through.

They returned to their human form. Dak saw the worried look on the pale faces of his men. "What has she done? She's separated the realms, trapping us here." Dak cried in disbelief.

Stephen moved toward the gate, touching the shimmering liquid. It rippled like a lake when a stone is tossed onto its smooth surface. His hand couldn't go through. "I didn't think this was possible."

"Nor did I," replied Dak. "It seems that my father underestimated the queen's powers."

"We can't just wait for her to return," Avis stated. "She will destroy us."

"We can't return to the city," Dak said. "We have to find a place to hide and prepare for her return."

They took the shape of smoke and traveled deep into the forest locating a cave in the mountainside and vanished inside. "Stay in the cave. I'm going to the castle to gather the things we will need to create a spell to shield us from her and to fight when she returns," Dak said.

"I'm going with you." Avis said. "We need supplies as well. We have no idea how long before her return."

Melting into smoke, they drifted toward the castle where they retook their shape inside. They split up. Avis vanished in a puff of smoke, reappearing in the kitchen. He quickly filled two dark bags with food. He searched through the cabinets for anything they could use.

Satisfied that he wasn't leaving anything useful behind, he hefted the bags over each shoulder and headed up the winding servant stairs. Eager to leave the castle, he looked around the grand hall before entering, and breathed a sigh of relief.

He didn't ever want to face Lady Mags again. King Ambro had no idea of the power she possessed.

Upstairs, Dak quickly made his way down the long decorative hall, his footsteps echoed off the cool stone floor. He opened and closed doors until he reached the end. He threw open the wide double door, and entered the Queen's chambers. His eyes darted around the cool blue room, coming to a stop at an ornate marble table.

He cautiously opened the crystal box in the center of the table, and smiled. He removed several glass vials and gently put them inside the pockets in the lining of his cloak.

As he started to shut the lid, all six of the vials had reappeared inside the crystal box. He frowned, quickly checked his pockets. The vials were still there.

Excited, he picked up the box and headed for the door. As he stepped through the threshold, the box disappeared. Startled, he jerked around and looked behind him. The crystal box was sitting in the middle of the table.

He quickly patted his pockets, relieved that the vials were still there. He raced down the long hallway to the graceful, marble, spiral staircase that led to the main hall.

Avis was pacing nervously back and forth at the bottom. Relief flooded his face when he saw Dak.

Dak joined Avis and picked up one of the dark bags. They couldn't turn to shadows with the bags, so they were forced to walk back to the cave. They walked through the deserted kingdom, across the sparkling blue river and into the woods without seeing or hearing any living creature.

The silence was unnerving. "Is every living thing in this realm a transformed human?" Avis asked.

"From what I've heard, yes. I think most of them shy away from eating other animals for this reason. Those that do eat meat hunt in the other realms." Dak explained.

Avis frowned. "If we can't eat meat, it will severely weaken us."

"I'm aware of that. One problem at a time. We prepare to defend ourselves for when she returns. I'm not sure what will be worse, her return, or staying away too long."

Pellgrino, the wanderer, met them at the entrance to the cave. He took the two bags and easily hefted them over his shoulder. "The cave runs deep underground, and in several directions. With a simple mist spell, it will be hard to locate us." He said.

Dak patted Grino warmly on the shoulder. "It will at least make it harder to locate us. Very well done my friend."

"I think we should explore these tunnels. They could lead to a way home." Avis said.

Dak didn't think there was a chance of that, but it wouldn't hurt to check it out. "Divide up into four groups. I'll gather some water…"

"There is a river that runs through the bottom of the cave." Grino interrupted.

"That's convenient." Dak laughed.

Dak and Avis followed Grino deep inside the cave. They joined the other dark ones next to the river. By the look on their pale faces, Dak could tell they were worried. "Well, this certainly didn't go as planned." Dak joked.

Oref didn't smile. "No, it didn't. What happened to the shapeshifters being weak and in need of a strong ruler?" he snarled.

Ettor, the defender stepped between Dak and Oref, defensively.

Stephen rose to his feet to stand next to Dak. "King Ambro couldn't have foretold this," he said.

"Then he should have attended the yearly celebrations so he'd have some idea of what we would be up against," Oref declared.

Dak put up his hand to silence Stephan and Ettor. "He's right. The King assumed much and sent us here blindly. He listened to the giants, who haven't attended the celebrations in my lifetime."

"At least they were right about how fertile this realm is." Stephen added to lighten the mood.

They all laughed. It was hard to be angry at kind hearted Stephen. Kind generous Stephen that had no place here.

"Ok, while you guys see if you can find a way home, I'll use a mist spell to conceal us, then I will see if I can use Lady Mags' potions to help us get out of here in case you aren't successful."

Stephen patted Dak on the back reassuringly before disappearing down one of the four tunnels.

Dak took a deep breath. He felt responsible for them all being trapped here. He should have tried harder to get his father to see the folly of his decision to invade another realm.

Ambro refused to believe that the Giants were using him for reasons they kept to themselves. Dak sighed deeply, and put his hands close together, leaving a few inches between them. A dark fog appeared between his hands, growing darker and thicker.

Dak released it toward the entrance to the cave. It swallowed up the entrance and every trace of the caves' exterior.

He carefully removed the vials from his pockets inside his cloak, setting them gently on the ground. Now if he only knew what they could do. With a heavy, troubled heart, he stared at the vials, wishing for a way to save his friends.

The vial filled with amber liquid started to shake slightly, then the vial with the rose-colored liquid started to glow. Dak looked at them in awe. For some reason he wasn't afraid. It seemed like they were trying to tell him something.

The blue vial shimmered and shook. Dak lifted the lid off each vial. A spell went through his mind. He carefully repeated it. The scent of lavender filled the air. Dak repeated the spell. A sense of rightness overwhelmed him and he repeated the spell again.

A gust of wind swirled around him. He instantly recognized it as one of the tornado's Lady Mags used to remove her people from the realm.

He repeated the spell over and over until a silence filled the cave. He jumped to his feet and transformed to his smoky form and searched the dark tunnels, traveling down each of the four passages. There wasn't a trace of his friends. He exhaled and smiled. They were safe. He was confident that the spell sent them home.

Chapter Five

The Dark Realm

The tornado dropped Stephen, Avis, Grino, Oref, and the other dark ones off next to the gate inside the Dark Realm. Somehow, they were home. They looked around frantically for Dak.

"How did we get here?" Avis asked stunned.

"Dak. Somehow he did this." Stephen stated.

"We need to inform the king." Oref added.

They vanished into a dark shadow and drifted across the dark desolate land. They traveled over dark murky rivers, dry withered fields, through the dead empty skeletal forest.

The land was rapidly dying. What little grass that covered the ground, was yellow and brittle. There wasn't any sign of life.

They returned to their human form at a dark weathered castle. The bricks were dark and gray to match the landscape. Burning torches flanked each side of the ornate wooded door. Single file they entered the dark building, taking form inside the dark throne room.

The walls were covered in blood red tapestries with the family crest of a blood red moon and an owl occupied the center of the wall. The stone floor was covered by a dark rug with the family crest in the center. Another rug covered the stairs leading up to an ornate gold throne. Seated on the throne was the King of the Dark Ones. He was a slightly older version of his son, Dak.

King Ambro's brows drew together in concern when he didn't see his son among the twelve men approaching him. "You've returned earlier than I expected. I trust the mission was a success?"

Ettor stepped forward and bowed slightly. "No, my king. It didn't go well."

King Ambro slowly rose to his feet and took one step toward Ettor. His dark eyes quickly scanned the torch lit room. "Where is Dak?"

Ettor didn't respond.

King Ambro searched the other dark ones faces. "Where is my son?" he yelled menacingly.

Stephen climbed the steps, stopping one step below the King. "Lady Mags removed everyone from the kingdom and sealed the gates."

King Ambro stumbled back a step. "That's not possible."

"My Lord, it is possible."

"Did you escape before she did this?"

"No, my Lord. We were trapped. Somehow Dak created a spell from Lady Mags' potions and sent us home."

The King's eyes widened in alarm. He quickly recovered. "Dak is trapped there, alone?"

"I'm afraid so." Stephen replied.

King Ambro turned his back on them and retook his throne. "We have to find a way to open the gates or recreate the spell that Dak used to send you home. Avis, bring me the Sorcerer.”

Avis bowed at the waist. “Yes, your Majesty.”

Avis turned into a shadow and quickly darted out of the castle, down the dark cobble stone streets, through the dark weathered buildings that looked as if they were about to fall down. He materialized in front of a small shop with a weathered wooden sign with Sorcerer burned into it.

He rapped loudly on the door, waited and knocked again.

“Stop that knocking. I’m coming,” said a hoarse voice from inside. A white haired old man with a beard almost to his waist threw open the door and glared at Avis. “What do I owe the pleasure of your visit pointy one?” laughed Egon.

Avis pushed past Egon. “Quiet you crusty old witch. The king wants to see you.”

Egon studied Avis with his light blue eyes. The intelligence behind those eyes studied Avis’ disheveled appearance and smiled. “What trouble has he gotten himself into now?”

"How …" began Avis before stopping to glare at Egon. "Come on old witch, let's go."

"Let me remind you, pointy one, I'm not at the beck and call of your king. I will accompany you, just to learn what mess he has created now."

"He is your king too old man." Avis reminded Egon.

"No, he is not my king. He appointed himself the king of this realm and then alienated it from all the other realms except the giants, and they jerk him around like a puppet on a string."

"You speak treason old man. King Ambro will kill you if he hears you speak of him this way."

Egon laughed. "Let him try pointy one. If he had any power over me, he would have destroyed me a long time ago."

Avis stared at the old sorcerer in surprise. He had no idea there was trouble between the king and the sorcerer. What else didn't he know? "Come on old man, enough already."

Egon laughed and slowly followed Avis out the door, down the dark street. Sorcerer's, witches, vampires, and werewolves, in their human form strolled past them as they made their way toward the castle.

Egon's comments made Avis more aware of the people he passed. A few nodded in his direction, while most greeted the sorcerer warmly. Avis silently studied the old man. Something was definitely going on.

Egon laughed loudly next to him. "What's the matter pointy one? What's this? You have no idea what's occurring around you."

Avis refused to be bated by Egon. "Can't you move any faster old man?"

"Hee, Hee, getting under your skin am I? Take a close look around my boy, you won't like what you see."

Avis slowed his pace and took a close look at the dark, run down town. He looked at the pale face of the young attractive witch that crossed the street to avoid him. "What's the matter with her?" he asked softly.

"Glad you asked pointy. They are slowly dying. The entire realm is. Why do you think the king sent you to invade Lady Mags' realm?"

"How do you know about that?" Avis asked alarmed.

"Not much goes on that I don't know about."

"What's happened? Why are they dying?"

"We all are. You too pointy. Your death will just take a little longer."

"Stop speaking in riddles and tell me how this is happening." Avis demanded gripping Egon by his cloak threatening to shake him. Out of the corner of his eye, he saw a crowd start to gather, heading in his direction. He released Egon. "I apologize. I meant you no harm. Please tell me what is happening."

Egon waved the crowd away, took Avis by the arm and pulled him into an alley. "The king has eyes in town. Long ago the king made a deal with the giants. Their magic is what turned our entire realm dark. Without sunlight, over the years the soil died, the water's turned foul and no living thing can survive."

"We can't survive in the sunlight. That must be why he did this." Avis defended.

"Guess again pointy. Back then, we had six hours of our version of daylight. It was bright enough to grow food and keep the fish in the stream alive, but not bright enough to hurt you, pointy."

"Then why change things? I don't understand."

"It was uncomfortable for you, but didn't hurt you. Back then, we also had a council made up of witches, sorcerer's, werewolves and pointy's. Ambro was power hungry, and thought the daylight gave the other members of the council an advantage. So he made a deal with the giants for eternal darkness, cut off all ties with the other realms, and here we are, slowly dying."

"How do we fix this?"

"That's a conversation for another day. Let's see what your king wants of me."

They hurried from the alley, picking up their pace, they quickly make their way to the castle. Once inside, Avis took Egon by the elbow and led him inside, stopping at the bottom of the stairs leading to the throne room.

King Ambro waved them forward. "Welcome Egon. It's been a long time my friend."

"Not long enough," laughed Egon.

King Ambro joined in his laughter, thinking Egon was teasing.

"What do I owe the honor of being summoned to court?"

"I need your help my old friend. My son is trapped in Lady Mags' realm."

Egon frowned, old friend indeed. "Trapped how?" he asked, even though he knew the answer. "What is wrong with the gate?"

Ambro exhaled sharply. "Lady Mags has locked them, trapping Dak in her realm. I need your help to rescue him."

Egon raised one eyebrow in surprise and slowly sat down on the carpeted stairs. "I had no idea that this could be done."

"Where are my manners? Avis, fetch Egon a chair, and send for refreshments. Then leave us to talk."

Avis bowed, and turned to leave. He wished he could stay and hear the tale the king was spinning. But the sly old sorcerer already knew the truth.

Avis returned moments later, placing a chair near the king's throne. Two serving girls brought trays with fresh meat and fruit and placed them before Egon and the king, helping Egon to his feet.

Egon's mouth watered at the sight of the fresh fruit. He couldn't remember the last time he'd seen, let alone eaten fresh fruit. He speared a grape with his fork and popped it into his mouth. Its sweet juices slid over his tongue. He sighed in pleasure. "You'll have to tell me which market you visit. Mine is poorly lacking."

King Ambro laughed, ignoring the question. "Now tell me, my wise friend, can you rescue my son?"

"My king, I know of no way to unlock what I didn't know could be locked."

"Is there a spell that can bring him home?"

Egon pretended to think while attempting to eat every morsel that had been placed in front of him. "I believe I've heard mention of an ancient spell that might retrieve him."

King Ambro clapped his hands. "Tremendous. I knew you could do it. Well, what are you waiting for? Bring him home."

"Your majesty, I've heard of the spell, but I do not know it," he lied. "I will have to search through my papers and books to see if its secrets are among their pages."

King Ambro frowned. "How long will this take? His life may be in danger. Holding my son prisoner is an act of war. I want him safely home before I teach Lady

Mags a lesson," he declared, having just come up with a way to explain the upcoming war.

"It will take as long as it takes." Egon stated, annoyed.

King Ambro jumped to his feet. "Then get to it old man."

Egon rose to his feet. "Very well your majesty."

"Avis," yelled the King. "Escort Egon home. If he requires anything, see that he gets it."

"Yes sire." Avis said bowing to the king. Avis took Egon's arm and escorted him from the room. "Well?" he asked.

"The time has come for you to make a choice, my young friend, stay here and slowly die, or join us and live."

"What about my friends, family… and Dak?"

"Gather your friends and family and meet me at the Eastern edge of town. Dak is out of my reach."

Avis pulled Egon to a stop at the palace gate. "But you told the king you have heard of a spell."

"I did, from you. That is why we must go now. Three hours, no more."

Avis nodded. "Why the alliance with the giants?"

Egon turned, "He's afraid of their magic. If they turned this realm dark, could they turn it light again? That could destroy your kind."

Avis frowned in understanding, and watched the old wizard fade from view. He took a deep breath and headed back toward the castle.

Chapter Six

The Divide

One by one, witches, sorcerers and werewolves packed up their belongings and vanished into the dead forest east of town.

Egon placed a heavy tome in a worn leather pouch. Extinguishing a lone candle, he exited his shop, locking the door for the last time.

He glanced around the dry empty street and slowly made his way down it to the edge of town.

He sighed deeply and turned to take one last look at the only home he'd ever really known in his long life.

Sadness threatened to overwhelm him. He didn't know if or when he'd ever return.

He squared his shoulders and continued walking. When he reached the edge of town, disappointment tore through his heart. There was no sign of Avis. How could he have been so wrong? Suddenly worried that the king's army could be moments behind him, he picked up his pace.

As he reached the edge of the dead forest, he was startled by men, women and children stepping out from behind the trees.

Avis grasped Egon's hand in his. "Sorry to startle you old witch." He said with respect. "We felt exposed out in the open."

Egon recognized Stephen, Ettor, Grino and the rest of the king's commanders. Oref was the only one missing. "Oref?" he asked.

"He sees the king's views on events."

"Let us go then. When you are missed, the king will rally his remaining army."

Avis laughed. "That will be a little more difficult with only one commander."

"He won't waste time replacing you. What they lack in skill they will make up in determination." Addressing the crowd of vampires, "Take your shadow form, and head due east until there is a break in the trees. I will meet you there."

"How?" Stephen asked.

Egon and his belongings vanished.

The crowd gasped as everything they carried vanished with him. Over one-hundred shadowy figures of different sizes and hues of black wove between the stark trees where they transformed back to their human shape at the end of the dead forest.

Egon and their belongings were waiting for them. They gathered them and followed Egon to the edge of a clearing. Egon turned and faced the crowd of vampires.

"Years ago, this land prospered and was fertile. King Ambro feared that the light made your people weak so he made a deal with the giants for a spell to rid the land of all light. Don't be afraid. The light may be a little uncomfortable to you, but it will not hurt you."

Before them, a giant fortress appeared out of the darkness. It lit up the land around them, pushing the darkness away.

The crowd of vampires gasped at the brightest light most of them had ever seen. Instinctively, they shielded their eyes from the light. Ganon, an older vampire made his way through the crowd to stand next to Egon. "What he says is true. I remember. Don't fear the light."

Nervously, the crowd followed Egon across the draw bridge. "Look mommy," cried a young girl "There's something in the water."

Ganon laughed, picked her up so she could get a better look. "They are fish. All the rivers and streams used to be full of them."

All the children and most of the adults couldn't resist looking down at the river filled with fish. As they enter the muted light, their skin tingled, but it wasn't unpleasant.

Inside, the massive gate closed behind them with a loud bang, startling the children. Their unease was quickly forgotten as they looked around them in awe. The fortress was enormous.

On one side, as far as the eye could see were orchards, vineyards and farms, all in full bloom. The air was crisp and clean. A blue jay flew by and landed on its nest in a tree.

"Is this heaven?" asked a small boy.

Egon picked the boy up, hugging him gently. "No lad, this is our home. This is what the realm used to look like."

"Why don't you restore the entire realm?" Stephen asked.

Egon sighed. "My magic isn't strong enough. It takes the magic of all the sorcerers to combat the giant's spell and keep us hidden. The living quarters are on the right. Please take what you need and meet in the great hall in an hour. You will need to elect a representative to sit on the council. Welcome to Opaque."

The great hall was filled with vampires, sorcerers, witches and werewolves in their human form. The vampires were hesitantly welcomed.

Egon sat at the highly polished round table, where he was quickly joined by the witch, Vestry, and the werewolf, Collin.

Avis quietly took his place having been voted to represent the vampires. Egon smiled in excitement. "This is the first time in more than a century that the council is complete. This is cause for celebration."

The crowd seated around the room erupted with cheering and applause. When the room grew quiet again, he continued. "King Ambro will send his army to find us, but he won't prevail. We are safe here and need to work and train together for the coming battle."

He picked up a worn wooden box off the floor next to him, setting it in front of him on the table. The crowd watched in silence as he opened the box, removed the contents that were covered with a pale blue cloth.

He pushed the box to the side and looked proudly around the packed room. "This is a proud moment for our people and this realm. This is a day that you will tell your children and grandchildren about."

He removed the blue cloth gently and revealed a smooth black stone. Avis glanced at the other members of the council and they looked as bewildered as he was. A blue light pulsed from the side of the stone facing Egon.

Yellow faced the werewolf, red in front of Avis and white for Vestry, the witch.

The colorful lights grew brighter and a beam of light suddenly shot out of the top of each stone. A five-pointed star appeared on the ceiling. The room was filled with an amber light, bathing the crowd with its warmth and strength.

Egon was noticeably stronger and healthier. Everyone could feel its healing strength wash over them. "As long as we are united, we can heal this land." Egon's voice boomed out. "We will train together, fight together, play together and live together as one."

Chapter Seven

Dak

Dak sat in front of a small fire. He was lost in thought. His face was drawn and worn. He had lost all track of time, having no idea how long he'd been hiding inside the cave.

He awoke a few days ago, certain that something was different. He used a spell to create food and finished his meal while trying to decide if he should leave the cave or continue to wait.

Tired of waiting, he extinguished the fire, and picked up his pack containing the crystal vials, throwing it over his shoulder.

In no hurry, he made his way to the front of the cave. It appeared to be darker than normal. Something had changed, which meant the gates could be open. He hefted the pack over his shoulder wondering if he should leave it behind, or risk getting caught by taking it with him.

The vials were too important for him to leave them behind. He looked past the mist hiding the caves' entrance. All was quiet. He felt someone searching for him. With a wave of his hand, he dispelled the mist and stepped outside. The breeze was warm on his face. He moved his hand in front of his face and down his body, rendering him nearly invisible.

He had made good use of his time in the cave to experiment with the liquid in the vials. Without hesitation, he darted away from the cave, stealthily making his way through the thick forest toward the gate and home.

Slade and Rhys immediately picked up his trail, the tracking spell allowing them to follow even what they were unable to see.

Dak picked up speed, weaving in and out of the trees. He could see the clearing and the silver blue light emanating from the gate. He stayed hidden at the fringe of the forest. Two men were guarding the gate. He watched them for a moment. He couldn't see any other guards.

They showed no sign that they detected his presence. He didn't think his cloaking spell would allow him to just walk up and through the gate without being noticed. His mind raced to come up with a plan. He extended his hands in front of him, mumbling a sleeping spell under his breath. He frowned in frustration and when nothing happened, he tried the spell again.

Still, nothing happened. "Damn." He muttered.

Slade and Rhys stood a few feet behind Dak. He had no idea that they were there. Together, they twirled a single finger in front of them. Unseen bonds wound their way around and around Dak, rendering him immobile.

Caught off guard, Dak didn't have a chance to react before a sleeping spell knocked him unconscious. They wrapped the dark cloak over him before picking him up and carrying him back to the castle.

Dak awoke much later, lying on a cot attached to a brick wall with a thick chain. He sat up and looked through the bars of his new home. "Well, that went well," he said to himself.

"Sorry to thwart your escape plans," Mags said, stepping out of the shadows.

"My Lady." Dak said. "I wish I could say that it is nice to see you."

Mags laughed. "I see you haven't lost your sense of humor."

"My wits and sense of humor are about all I have left."

"Your belongings will be returned to you. Minus the things you took from my room."

Dak rose to his feet to face Mags, his hands gripped the bars separating them. "They came in quite handy. I doubt I would have survived without them."

"I'm sure you found them very useful. I'm impressed, not many can master using the vials."

Dak shrugged. "They kind of helped me."

Mags wasn't quick enough to mask her surprise.

Dak raised his brows in interest. "From your reaction, I gather that isn't normal."

"It's normal, it just doesn't happen very often. The potions see something in you."

"Something good I hope," he teased.

"Yes, something good. I hope nothing has happened to your men. We can't find any trace of them."

"Your potions helped me to send them home. Unfortunately, they didn't show me how to go with them."

Her brows drew together in thought. The potions helped him and wanted him to stay. They had never been wrong. "How unfortunate. Our people have lived in peace for centuries. Why did you attempt to attack my realm?"

Dak winced at her choice of words even though he knew it could barely be called an attempt. "We received word that you were planning an attack since we haven't participated in the council for generations."

"While I admit that was a grievous mistake made by your father, the other realms didn't interfere with your choice. Why, after all this time would we have reason to intervene?"

Dak recognized the wisdom of her words. "It sounded better coming from my father." He admitted. "So, what now?"

"I've put a binding spell on you. You won't be able to leave the realm until it is removed. She put a gold key in the lock and opened the cell door.

"Why are you doing this?" he asked stopping next to her, looking deep into her eyes.

"Sending you home to regroup so you can attack my people again seems out of the question."

"But setting me free…"

"You're not free. You can't leave. That is a prison of sorts."

"A very gilded prison."

"You will be my guest so we can get to know one another so you can return home and assure your father that we pose no threat to him."

"That is more than fair my lady."

"I would also like to explore the fact that my potions see something special in you."

Dak is taken aback by her generosity. "Thank you. I would like that as well."

"Good. I will show you to your room, then you can join us for dinner."

"I am truly overwhelmed by your generosity." Dak was surprised to realize that he meant it. He truly had no desire to return home just yet, and he was very eager to learn more about the magic the potions could teach him.

He followed Mags up the carpeted stairs and down a long hallway. They exited the hallway into a large room.

Tiny butterfly people flew past them without a glance in their direction. Mags watched them go with a smile on her beautiful face. There were people and animals moving through the large room decorated in reds and blacks. They smiled and said hello as they passed Mags and Dak.

Dak was overcome by their friendliness. Mags led him up another staircase covered with a thick silver rug with pictures of animals woven in the rich fabric. She led him to the end of the hall and opened the door so he could enter. Sunlight filled the room. Dak stepped back instinctively.

"It's all right. I've put a filter on the amount of sunlight that enters the castle. It won't hurt you."

"How can you be sure?"

"Long ago your realm was divided between day and night, just like this realm, only the days were shorter. The sunlight was filtered just like this and didn't hurt you." She explained. "As long as you are on the castle grounds, the sunlight won't hurt you."

Dak's mind was racing. This can't be true. Who would turn his home into the dark miserable place it was if they could survive the sunlight. Hesitantly, he entered the room. He stuck his hand out and slowly let the sun shine on his fingertips. They tingled for a second, but it didn't burn him.

He slowly stepped into the light for the first time in his life. The sun was warm on his face. It was the most amazing thing he'd ever felt. He turned to Mags. "Thank you," he said, his voice filled with emotion.

Mags smiled warmly. She could tell that he was overwhelmed by the experience. "Dinner is in an hour. I'll send someone up to show you the way."

Dak nodded and continued to soak up the sun. He stood in front of the window, content to feel the sun's warmth on his skin until he heard a slight tapping on the door nearly an hour later. He crossed the room, looking at the richly decorated room for the first time.

A large bed occupied the center of the room covered in a rich brown comforter interwoven with gold. Twin night tables framed the bed with decorative figurines of animals standing proudly in the center.

The carpet was a plush beige that absorbed his footsteps as he crossed the room to open the door to meet the gazed of a beautiful butterfly girl. Well, he assumed it was a girl.

Her tiny face framed her big blue eyes. Her gossamer wings were pink and purple. She met his gaze and smiled. "Hi, I'm Iera. I'm here to escort you down to dinner," she said in a soft musical voice.

"Pleased to meet you Iera. I'm Dak …."

Iera giggled. "Silly, we all know who you are. Follow me, if you can keep up," she challenged.

Dak took his shadowy form and followed Iera through the hallway, out a window, across the courtyard, back through a window and into the main room. Dak returned to his human form and Iera landed on his shoulder and whispered in his ear. "Great job keeping up," and kissed him gently on the cheek.

She flew off and led him into the dining hall. Dak smiled and realized that was the first time he could remember feeling completely carefree. He followed Iera into the large dining room filled with tables covered in foods he didn't recognize.

Lady Mags waved at him from across the room aglow with candles burning overhead in crystal chandeliers. A roaring fire took up half of one wall and bathed the room in a warm glow. He passed by the fireplace and couldn't feel any heat coming from it.

Mags noticed him studying the fireplace as he took a seat next to her. "It's too warm for a fire, so I took the heat away, but I love how cozy and relaxing it is."

For the first time he noticed Sierra sitting to the right of Mags. There was something very different about her. There was no denying that she was pretty, and she had the darkest blue eyes he had ever seen. They seemed to see down to his soul.

Sierra quickly looked away from his intense scrutiny.

"Dak, this is Sierra. She too is my guest." Mags said.

Dak raised one eyebrow. Did that mean she was a prisoner here too? He wondered what she did. "It's my pleasure to meet you, my lady," he said.

"It's nice to meet you too." Sierra replied.

Dak studied her more closely. He couldn't place her accent.

"She isn't from here." Mags said as a simple explanation.

Exactly what did that mean? She's not from here.

Uncomfortable under Dak's scrutiny, Sierra helped herself to a salad with some leaves she didn't recognize. She piled her plate with an assortment of vegetables, aware that Dak continued to watch her.

Dak was served a plate with meat and vegetables. He nodded his head in appreciation to Mags. Dak looked over at Sierra and asked, "What exactly does that mean, you're not from here? What realm are you from?"

Sierra's gaze darted to Mags.

Mags smiled. "She isn't from any of the eight realms."

Dak found this unbelievable. "I wasn't aware there was anything beyond the eight realms. How did you get here?"

Mags frowned slightly. "I brought her here."

Dak didn't miss the frown and dropped the issue. "I would love to hear about your home." Dak said to Sierra.

"I think it is a wonderful idea for you two to get to know each other." Mags suggested.

The remainder of the meal was eaten in silence except for bits of small talk between Mags and other people sitting at the table.

The butterflies brought out individual, tiny, elaborately decorated tarts for each guest. Sierra studied the tiny work of art that resembled the flowers on a honeysuckle. She popped the tiny creation in her mouth and the sensation was indescribable.

It was sweet, but not too sweet. First it tasted like caramel, then quickly changed to strawberry, lemon, cherry and then fresh blackberry cobbler. "That is amazing," she exclaimed.

Dak put his tiny dessert that resembled a dragonfly on his tongue. It tasted like sugared pecans, then rum cake, then a sweet confection from his realm that he hadn't tasted in years, called an isar, and lastly a tart lemon pudding. "I agree. This is amazing."

Mags smiled warmly. "I'm glad you enjoyed it. They are different for everyone. It is a very special treat created by the butterflies. I will let them know that you approve."

A gentle rap on Sierra's door interrupted her wandering thoughts. She opened the heavy oak door to see one of the butterfly people smiling at her. "Good morning miss," greeted Sim, a handsome dark-haired butterfly.

"Good morning." Sierra replied. She'd never seen a male butterfly person before. Laughing to herself, she thought that it only made sense for there to be male and female.

"I'm Sim. I will escort you to Lady Mags' room."

"Thank you."

Sierra gently shut the door behind her and noticed a beautiful butterfly knocking on what she assumed was Dak's room. She turned away and followed Sim. His orange and yellow wings reminded her of the sunrise.

Dak heard the soft knock on his door and moved away from the window, and out of the sunlight. "Good morning Iera," he said opening the door.

"Do you think you can keep up again?" she teased, and took off.

Dak shed his physical form and followed her down the hall and out an open window. They flew around the castle, and climbed up the stone wall and in through another window.

Iera stopped suddenly and Dak covered her with his shadowy form, inches away from Mags. Iera coughed and Dak took his human form. Dak smiled weakly at Mags. He was afraid that he was getting off to a bad start.

He turned and glared at Iera who floated next to his shoulder. She shrugged and smiled.

Mags burst out laughing. "I wish that the two of you could see your faces. Iera, couldn't you have shown him in through the door?"

"What's the fun in that?" she laughed and took off out the window.

"I apologize Lady Mags. I …"

"Don't apologize," she interrupted. "There's nothing wrong with having a little fun. I'm glad I had time to get dressed before you two burst into the room."

Sim led Sierra into the room halting their conversation. How did he beat her here? Then she remembered that he could transform into a shadow. "Good morning Lady Mags, Dak," she said.

"Please call me Mags. After all I was your pet for years," she teased. "You too Dak, Mags from now on."

"Yes ma'am," he said, smiling. "Her pet?"

"That's a story for another time. We are going to explore your magical abilities today."

Sierra looked at Mags in surprise. Why would she teach Dak magic? After all, he did try to take over her kingdom.

Dak looked at Sierra and winked.

"You both possess hidden magical abilities that I'd like to bring out."

It was Dak's turn to be surprised. He was curious as to where Sierra came from and what existed beyond the eight realms.

Mags crossed the room and picked up an ornately carved box and placed it on a small table near the window. She motioned for them to join her. As they surround the table, Mags opened the box. Nestled inside the velvet lined box were six crystal vials.

Dak recognized them as the same vials that he had stolen from Mags. He grinned sheepishly at her.

Mags laughed. Sierra recognized them as the same potions Mags used to clear the darkness. "Dak, as long as you remain worthy, these potions belong to you. Use them wisely. If you use them selfishly or for evil, they will disappear." Mags said.

"I don't understand." Dak said in confusion. After what he tried to do, to be given such an amazing gift was beyond understanding.

"The potions see the good in you. I have faith that they will help you find it in yourself."

"Thank you for your kindness and belief in me. I will do my best to not disappoint you."

"I expect you to succeed." Mags moved over to the marble table containing her potions. She pulled an ivory box out of nothing and sat it on the table next to her crystal box. She opened the lid and smiled at Sierra. "I want you to choose six potions. Don't just choose them randomly. Wait for them to connect to you."

"What if they don't connect?" Sierra asked.

"Then they will not work for you. Relax, clear your mind and think of nothing except for the crystals in front of you."

Sierra nodded. She tried to block out Dak standing to her left. She could feel his eyes on her. She looked down at the delicate crystal box with at least twenty colorful potions in crystal decanters.

Concentrating, the room around her faded from view. She no longer felt Dak watching her. All she could see were the crystal decanters in front of her. Even the table seemed to have vanished. A vial with a teal liquid seemed to glow. Sierra reached out and picked it up.

Mags took it from her and placed it in the ivory box. Sierra quickly picked five more vials. Mags took them and put them gently in the box. Sierra felt a warmth wash over her filling her with an energy like nothing she'd ever felt before.

The room started to come back into focus. She blinked twice so she could see the room clearly again. Dak and Mags were standing across the table from her, staring.

"Did I do something wrong?" she asked.

Mags patted her hand resting on the cool surface of the table reassuringly. "No, my dear. Are you all right?"

Sierra looked at Dak then at Mags. They were still looking at her oddly. "Yes, why? Did something happen?"

"You glowed." Dak said so softly she wasn't sure she heard him correctly.

"I what?"

"You started to glow after I took the last potion from you." Mags added.

"I only remember picking up the first potion." Sierra said.

"That's perfectly all right. You connected with them very strongly. After lunch I will teach you to communicate with them," she laughed. "Well, I think you've both already done that, but we will refine your method. Enjoy lunch and we will resume." Mags instructed, waving them off.

"Lunch, we just got here," Sierra said in surprise

Dak laughed. "It took you over three hours to pick your potions."

Sierra looked at Mags and she nodded, confirming what Dak said.

Sierra and Dak made their way down the stairs in silence. They entered the dining hall and were immediately greeted by several cheerful fluttering butterflies.

They quickly placed small plates of food that took three of them to carry onto the table in front of them. Sierra eyed the thin slices of pot roast on Dak's plate and speared a slice with her fork, popping it into her mouth.

Dak's eyes widened with amusement. Sierra smiled with pleasure. "That is so good," she exclaimed. "I'm sorry, but I'm a little tired of fruits and vegetables."

Dak burst out laughing and put two slices of roast on her plate. "It will be our little secret."

Sierra quickly glanced around the room and slowly savored the succulent beef.

"So, tell me about the realm you come from."

"We don't call it a realm, but it is very different from here. We don't have magic, but we have technology that some could call magic."

"No magic? How very odd that must be. Is it a big place?"

"Very big. We do very well without magic."

"But you have magic, maybe others do as well and don't know it."

"I've thought about that. I think that my being here has brought out the magic in me."

Dak raised one eyebrow. "That could be true."

"Tell me about your realm."

Dak frowned. "It's dark and dying. That's why my father sent me here to take over this realm. He wasn't quite truthful about a few things," he said sadly.

"Like what?"

Dak looked down ashamed. "He said Mags was cruel and excluded us from the council, and it was her fault that our realm was dying."

"That doesn't sound like Mags."

"I know; which means my father lied to me and I want to know why."

Sierra covered his hand with hers. "I'm sorry about your dad."

Dak looked deep into Sierra's dark blue eyes. The kindness he saw there was foreign to him. He covered her hand with his. "You don't think I'm a monster for what I did?"

Sierra frowned sadly. "Of course not. You were helping your people. I admire that."

"He told me that the other realms consider us monsters," he said sadly, lowering his head.

"Has anyone here treated you like a monster?"

"No, they have been more than kind. I don't understand my father's lies."

"Tell me about your people. Where I come from you are a mythical creature that drains the blood from people turning them into vampires."

Dak is surprised that her world knows of his kind, even as a myth. "I believe that hundreds of years ago, my ancestors were blood drinkers, but trust me, we can't turn anyone into one of us. I wonder if we have visited your world during our blood thirsty era."

"I guess anything's possible. I'm here. Is everyone in your realm is a vampire?"

"No. We have werewolves, witches and sorcerers as well."

Sierra's eyes widened in surprise. "Sounds like the perfect ingredients for a horror movie," she laughed teasingly.

Dak looked at her in confusion. "Horror movie? I'm afraid I don't understand."

Sierra frowned. How could she explain a movie? "Where I'm from, we capture images on film and they tell a story. It is played on a big white screen." She studied his face to see if that made any sense to him.

Dak's dark eyes turned darker. "And if my kind were in this movie it would be a horror?" he said angrily pulling his hand away from hers.

Sierra grabbed his hand, clenching it between hers, pulling it back toward her. "I'm so sorry. Movies about vampires are usually scary, but I didn't mean to insult you. They are not real where I'm from."

Dak put her hand over his heart. "We are very real my lady." He took a deep breath and smiled. "And sometimes we can be very scary."

Sierra sighed with relief. "You forgive me? I truly didn't mean to insult you."

"I will forgive you, if you tell me how it was to have lady Mags as your pet," he laughed.

Sierra smiled, removing her hand that was pressed flat against his chest. "She was a very naughty cat, always getting into trouble. She liked to kill birds and bring them to me."

Dak laughed. "You better not tell her that," he said looking up to see Mags standing a few feet away.

Mags clutched her hand to her chest. She was pale and looked stricken.

Sierra jumped to her feet and escorted her to a chair. "Are you all right? Can I get you anything?"

Mags shook her head, a single tear slid down her smooth cheek.

"What's the matter Mags?" Dak asked, growing concerned for her.

"What if they were one of my people?" She said tearfully.

"Who?" Sierra asked confused.

"The birds."

Dak tried to stifle his laughter, but failed miserably.

Sierra pushed him so hard he nearly fell out of his chair. He waved his arms frantically, looking like he was trying to fly, instead of regaining his balance. He righted the chair with a thud and looked at Sierra and Mags.

They burst out laughing at the same time. Dak joined in their laughter. Mags waved her hand in front of her face attempting to regain her composure. "It's not funny."

Dak and Sierra tried to get their laughter under control. Sierra was crying from laughing so hard.

"Are you missing anyone?" Dak asked.

Mags searched her memory and replied, "I don't believe so. And no one has been reported missing. I'm so relieved," she added.

"Then your conscience is clear. You didn't eat one of you subjects." Dak said with amusement.

Mags frowned and Sierra and Dak struggled not to laugh.

Chapter Eight

Magic Lessons

Mags put Sierra and Dak on the opposite side of her bed room. Their boxes sat open in front of them on marble tables. Sierra was nervous and excited. She had no idea what to expect while Dak was eager to get started.

"Even though you've used your potions before, Dak, we are going to start slow." Mags explained. "Listen to the potions. They will tell you what to do. The more you are in harmony with them, the more powerful your magic."

A crystal bowl appeared on each table. "Your first task is to create snow. Take your time and concentrate."

Sierra stared at the box in front of her. Like before, she closed off everything around her. She picked up two potions and poured a small amount from each into the bowl.

She was slightly distracted when the vials refilled themselves. She concentrated again, waving her hand over the pale liquid. A small cloud formed in the bowl and floated up toward the ceiling, and started snowing. Delighted she looked over at Mags, then at Dak.

They were standing knee deep in pink snow. Sierra felt foolish, then shrugged it off and laughed.

"Dak is a little over eager." Mags said laughing. "Nice work Sierra. That is more what I had in mind."

Sierra smiled. "Is snow pink here?" she asked.

Mags and Dak laughed. "According to Dak it is." Dak frowned and shrugged.

"Dak was kind enough to give an example of what happens if you don't concentrate." Mags teased.

"Whatever." Dak remarked, smiling mischievously.

"You both did very well." Mags said. With a wave of her hand, Dak's snow disappeared.

"How did you do that?" Dak asked.

"I can't teach you that. You either possess the ability or you don't."

Sierra frowned. "How do you know if you possess it?"

"If you possess the magic you will know it soon."

Sierra turned and looked at Dak. "You can do magic?" She asked.

"Mine is very limited compared to what Mags can do."

"Maybe you can strengthen your magic as well." Mags suggested. "Now next task, I want you to create a bouquet of flowers."

Sierra created a bouquet of lavender roses. Dak chose a black and yellow flower that looked like an orchid. He explained that it used to grow in his realm when he was a child. Mags led them through one task after another. Creating objects from the potions became easier with each task.

While Sierra and Dak were distracted congratulating each other, Mags shot tiny ice crystals at them to gage their reaction.

Dak immediately countered them with a puff of wind and blew them harmlessly away. He extended the wind to blow them away from Sierra too.

Startled, Sierra created a bubble of energy around her. Mags and Dak stared at her in disbelief. Dak slowly approached her. He reached out and touched the field surrounding Sierra. He felt a slight tingle, but it didn't hurt.

Sierra noticed the energy field in front of her and gasped, stepping back in surprise. The field disappeared. She realized that Dak and Mags were looking at her strangely. "What was that?" she asked in surprise.

Dak and Mags shared a strange look between them.

"What?" Sierra asked. Her eyes widened. "No. It's not possible. I didn't do that."

Mags quickly crossed the room, taking Sierra's hands between hers. She gently led her over to a plush green sofa, and pulled her down onto it. "I'm so sorry. I didn't mean to frighten you." She apologized.

"You both were doing so well in your training that I wanted to see how well you would react to a threat."

Dak sat on the other side of Sierra and put his hand reassuringly on her shoulder. "But how? I don't understand. There isn't magic in my world."

Mags sighed. "There is magic in your world. They've just forgotten it. It may have reawakened in you by being here."

"There is nothing to be afraid of," Dak added.

Sierra turned and smile at him. "Thanks for protecting me."

"I'm pretty sure you didn't need it, but you are most welcome."

Chapter Nine

Prepare for Battle

Egon watched from across the cobblestone courtyard as vampires, werewolves and witches, dressed in loose cotton shirts and leather training breaches tucked into soft leather boots, trained together in combat. The sorcerer stood off to the side casting spells for them to counter and ward off.

His gaze moved past their practice field to the lush green farmland filled with vegetables ripe and ready for harvest. He smiled, excited at how well everything was going. He was hopeful that they would be ready in time for what was coming. He was pleased at how well the vampires, witches and werewolves were training side by side.

King Ambro entered his ornate throne room. He looked around the dark room, shadows dancing in the corners. The white tapered candles burning in the chandelier overhead did little to dispel the gloom. He frowned slightly, wondering where everyone was. His commanders were usually in attendance by now.

He saw Oref enter the great room and motioned for him to join him. Oref quickly crossed the room. "Where is everyone?" Ambro asked.

Oref recalled the strange conversation he had with Avis regarding the king not being honest with them. He suddenly became concerned for his friend. If the king had done something to him, he wouldn't be asking where they were. He exhaled sharply. "I will see if I can locate them."

"Take someone with you."

Oref nodded and hurried out, his shoes tapping on the hardwood floor. He exited the castle, his gaze moved to the left across the empty practice field surrounded by a worn wooden fence.

He slowly made his way across the dry packed ground, following the fence line to the guard house where all the king's soldiers lived. He opened the heavy wooden door, startling the soldiers awake as the door creaked loudly when he opened it.

They jumped to their feet as he entered the dimly lit room. He noticed immediately that half of the beds were unoccupied.

He selected Aris, a young girl with big dark eyes and a quick smile, and Ramon, a strong fighter with a big heart. They followed Oref outside and through the castle to the commanders training room. It was just as he'd left it the day before. Frowning, he left the room and searched the commanders living quarters upstairs.

The rooms were neat. He opened the closet in Avis' room and noticed that some of his clothes were missing. It was the same in the other rooms. Where could they be?

Worried, concerned and uneasy he hurried down the hall to the main staircase. He took the stairs two at a time. Aris and Ramon easily kept pace with him. They hurried out of the castle, down the cobblestone path toward the village.

Oref slowed his pace as he neared the village shops. All the windows were dark. The streets were deserted and quiet.

"Where is everyone?" Aris asked.

Oref looked around in bewilderment. "I have no idea."

"Do you think it's the giants?" Ramon asked.

"Why would the giants take our people?" Oref asked.

"Who else could do something like this?" Ramon said.

"Lady Mags." Oref whispered. "Follow me."

Oref turned to a shadow as did Aris and Ramon. He rushed through town, delighted to see several vampires moving through the streets, opening up shops. They moved past them and materialized in front of the shimmering gate, deep inside the dead forest. He put his hand on the smooth surface of the gate and was surprised when his hand went through. The gates were open again. He turned back into a shadow and rushed back toward the castle.

As they raced through the town Oref saw a few werewolves and witches setting up their shops. Relief flooded over him at the sight of them and he materialized in front of them. Avis and Ramon followed suit. "Where is everyone?" Oref asked the old witch, Minerva as she waved her hand over a basket and filled it with juicy red grapes.

Minerva cackled loudly. "They're all gone."

"I can see that. Where have they gone?"

"They took to the forest."

"Make sense old woman."

"They all left. The land is dying. Everything is dying," she laughed.

"What do you mean that everything is dying? Why are you still here?"

She laughed. "Look around you boy. It's all dead."

Oref stared at her and decided she was crazy. He was wasting time talking to her. He motioned for Aris and Ramon to follow him. They entered a weathered old shop, run by an old werewolf. Aris glanced at the dainty soaps and lotions on his shelves.

Oref frowned, surprised to see the items he was selling. "Good day. How may I help you?" Patrick, the owner, asked.

Aris picked up a bar of scented soap and smelled it. Vanilla, she smiled. "Your soap smells wonderful."

"Thank you. A lady giant fancies them. Keeps my business thriving."

"How fortunate," Oref said. "Can you tell me where everyone is?"

"They didn't divulge their plans to me. I doubt they would trust me. After all, I associate with the giants."

"The witch Minerva said everyone just left? Where would they go?"

"Again, I wouldn't know."

Frustrated, Oref vanished in a puff of smoke, racing down the nearly empty streets toward the castle.

Aris smiled at Patrick, vanished, the bar of soap dropped to the floor. Ramon followed quickly behind her.

Patrick picked up the bar of soap and smiled.

Oref materialized in the great hall and walked quickly toward the king. King Ambro nodded to Oref. "Back so soon. Did you locate them?"

"No, your majesty, and the town is nearly deserted. An old witch said they left because everything is dying."

King Ambro tried to hide his surprise and the fear that raced through him. The old witch told him this would happen, but it was too soon. His commanders couldn't have willingly left. He needed them. "Dying? What does she mean? We're not dying."

"The gates are opened again. Do you think Lady Mags took our people?"

King Ambro smiled on the inside, wonderful idea. Blame Lady Mags. "She could have. After all, she is holding Dak prisoner. If she is declaring war on us, we will need the giant's help. Take your two new recruits and seek out the giants to us help bring our people home."

Oref motioned for Aris and Ramon to follow before turning to smoke. He raced back through town, through the dead forest to the gate leading to the giant's realm. He passed through the gate with Aris and Ramon right behind him, stopping on the other side protected by a thick dark screen.

They could see the sun setting in the distance and waited for it to disappear. "It's beautiful." Aris said wistfully, admiring the pink and yellow sun setting in the deep blue sky.

"And deadly to us," Oref reminded her.

King Ambro slowly strolled to the guard house. The guards jumped to their feet when they saw him enter. They bowed their heads in respect. "Please, raise your heads. It seems as if we are in the midst of dire times. Many of our people have disappeared. I fear that Lady Mags has taken them."

He paused to give them time to absorb his words. "I need you to gear up and prepare for war. Choose four leaders and prepare for battle."

"Yes sir." They said in unison.

King Ambro smiled and left, making his way across the courtyard where he was confronted by Minerva.

"It's happening, and there is nothing you can do to stop it," she taunted.

King Ambro tried to wave her away, but his limited magic was useless on her. "Be gone old witch."

"Your time is at an end. You have a choice to make, but knowing you, you'll make the wrong one again."

"Leave me in peace old woman."

"You know Mags didn't take your people. You know exactly where they are."

King Ambro walked around her, ignoring her and continued toward the castle.

She appeared in front of him. "You will not like the outcome old fool," she said, then disappeared.

— ❖ —   — ❖ —   — ❖ —

Egon continued to watch his people practice, with pride. They put aside their differences and trained together smoothly. He was so proud of how everyone came together so quickly. Spiriva, an attractive younger female sorcerer appeared in front of him, startling him.

"The king is enlisting the giant's aid to attack Lady Mags. He believes that she's responsible for our disappearance."

Egon frowned. "Thank you. Keep me informed. We can't do anything to help Lady Mags. We are not ready yet. We need more time," he said sadly.

Chapter Ten

The Giants

Aris, Ramon and Oref waited and watched the sun set behind the snow-covered mountain. The valley was green and teaming with life. Colorful birds flew overhead and a small red fox cautiously approached them. He sniffed the air, then ran away.

"It is beautiful here," Aris said. "I see why the witch said our realm is dying," she added.

"One problem at a time," Oref said. He had to admit to himself that she was right. Everything in their realm was dead, not dying, dead. Not one plant, tree or animal remained. Maybe the people were leaving too.

"I think it is safe for us to go," Ramon said. "Which way?"

Oref frowned. "I have no idea. I have never been to the giant realm before."

"I have," Aris said. "I've been hunting several times. The city is to the east, or so I've been told."

"You've never been there?" Ramon asked.

"No, and I'd rather not go now. I don't trust the giants, but we have no choice. Let's get this over with," Aris said. "They don't like us very much from what I hear. They also don't like us to be in our shadowy form. Seems like everything we do angers them.

"I wonder how we ever got them to sign a treaty with us," Oref added. The three of them turned to shadows and headed east across a meadow filled with golden flowers. Their fragrant sent was the sweetest thing any of them had ever smelled. The meadow ended at the edge of a town with the tallest building they had ever seen. Materializing, they slowly headed inside, looking around them in awe.

They noticed that the homes on the edge of town were smaller. The larger, nicer homes were nearer the town square. The smaller homes were made of mud bricks and stood forty feet high. Aris shuddered to think how big, even the smaller giants were. She would be glad when their business was concluded and they could return home.

They walked past the smaller houses and reached the second level of homes before they saw a giant. He was nearly twenty feet tall with bright red hair. His skin was a pale pink, burned from the sun. He didn't see the three vampires as they hid behind a tree.

They waited until he went inside before continuing down the street. "They are so big," Aris exclaimed softly.

"He's not even one of the tallest," Oref said.

They made it to the center of the city when a blond, thirty feet tall giant stood in their path. "Did your king send you to see Marcus?" asked Treynor in a soft musical voice.

Oref, Aris and Ramon exchanged looks of surprise. "Yes. We need to speak with Marcus," Oref replied.

"Follow me," he instructed. They had to run to keep up with him. Treynor pushed open a massive wooden door, holding it open so they could enter. The room was the size of Ambro's castle. Each tile was the size of a house. The room was vacant, not even curtains covered the enormous floor to ceiling windows.

"Wait here," he said.

They waited expectantly, eager to speak to the giant leader. A dark-haired giant, around twenty-five feet tall entered the room and quickly crossed it to join them. He gently sat down on the floor next to them. "King Ambro sent you?" he asked in a deep voice.

"Yes. He sent us to ask for your help." Aris said.

"Help with what?"

"Most of the villagers have disappeared." Aris added.

"I know nothing of your villagers."

"We are afraid Lady Mags has taken them," Oref explained.

Marcus raised one massive eyebrow. "Why on earth would she do that?"

"She is holding Prince Dak prisoner in her realm since the gates reopened," Oref said, avoiding telling the entire story.

"While I haven't been to Mags' court in many a year, this doesn't sound like something she would do."

"She may have changed since her return." Oref said.

"What does the king want from us?"

"We plan to do whatever it takes to bring our people home," Avis said.

"And you want us to join you?"

"Yes. We are in need of your help," Oref said.

"I will discuss your request with my council and send a missive with my decision."

Oref bowed his head in respect. "Thank you. How long do you expect it to be before you have an answer?"

"As long as it takes. I will send my response when it has been decided."

"Thank you."

"Please show them out Treynor."

"Follow me," Treynor instructed. They followed him back outside.

Night had fallen when Treynor left them outside the massive building.

"I'm not sure that went well," Aris said.

"Me either," Oref agreed. "Since it is dark and they won't be able to see us if we transform. Let's get out of this place."

"Why does our transforming offend them?" Ramon asked.

"Who knows, but I don't really care right now. Keep to the shadows."

They moved away from the front of the building, transformed and floated away, keeping to the shadows as they moved through the tall dark buildings framing the empty streets. The town appeared deserted.

⁕ ⁕ ⁕

Marcus sank into a thick plush chair facing a corner hidden by shadows. "What did they want?" asked Raylynn, her voice soft and sultry.

"They think that Lady Mags has taken their villagers and want our help to get them back."

"Interesting," she purred.

"You aren't considering helping them?"

"Why not? You know how I feel about Mags," Raylynn said.

"Yes, but you and I both know she had nothing to do with the disappearances of the villagers."

"But, you've always known that I want to confront Mags. It might help us to have the vampires there as a distraction."

"Letting your emotions make a decision for you isn't wise." Marcus reminded her.

She laughed a deep throaty laugh. "You know me too well."

"That I do."

"We need a practice run before we encounter Mags. Get everything together for a trial run, then we will send King Ambro a message."

"As you wish," Marcus said.

The missive was delivered hours later, by a fat blue and gray hummingbird. He dropped it in King Ambro's hand and raced away. The King smiled as he read that a small giant army would arrive and assist in discovering the whereabouts of the missing villagers.

He would get his people back, then he would get his son.

⁕ ⁕ ⁕

Within the hour of the arrival of the missive, twelve giants, standing over twenty feet tall stood outside the castle. There footsteps sounded like thunder, rousing Ambro, half asleep on his throne. Ambro slowly climbed to his feet, and looked around the empty throne room in disgust.

He had to locate his people. There was barely any kingdom left for him to rule. He pulled a whistle out of the interior of his robe and blew out two shrill notes.

Oref entered through a door across the room. "Yes, your majesty."

"Gather the troops and join me outside. Reinforcements have arrived."

"Yes, your majesty," he said bowing slightly at the waist.

King Ambro threw open the door, happy and disappointed to see the twelve giants staring down at him. He had expected an army of giants, but these would have to do. "Welcome to the Dark Realm," Ambro said eagerly.

Treynor stepped forward, shaking the ground as he moved. "Let's get on with this. I'd rather not stay in this wretched realm any longer than we have to."

Ambro frowned seething with anger. How dare he insult him like that. He wouldn't forget it.

Treynor jerked his head around. "I sense strong magic." He turned and headed toward town. The other giants immediately followed him. They stomped their way through the village. The vibrations from their steps rattling windows, and shaking the fragile walls of the worn, weathered buildings, causing shingles to crash to the street below. If they noticed, they didn't care to slow their pace to avoid damaging the town.

The vampires followed at a distance in their shadowy form.

Treynor glanced back at the shadowy forms following them and frowned in disgust. He didn't like the vampires.

They crashed through the dead trees and came to an abrupt stop.

The vampires took their solid form and moved in front of the giants. They looked around the desolate area in confusion, but remained quiet, waiting expectantly. Under his breath Treynor murmured repeatedly. "Ashna aloas nemna."

Oref and the king's army watched in wonder as a fortress appeared in front of them. The black fortress towered above the trees and above the giants.

The giants looked up at the massive battlements in surprise. An unfamiliar flag snapped in the breeze at the top of the tallest tower.

The vampires drew back in fear at the light that filled the forest. The wall surrounding the fortress was taller than the giants but they could see the healthy fruit trees over the top of the fortress walls.

"What is this place?" Aris asked in bewilderment. She stepped closer into the light. It stung a bit, but to her surprise, it didn't hurt.

Ramon cried out, "Get back."

Aris turned to face them. "It's all right. It doesn't hurt. It's so warm," she said in wonder. She moved closer and stared down at the clear blue water filled with fish. She bent down and touched the cool water. "It's beautiful."

The remaining army joined her next to the river. They had never seen clean water outside of a glass, let alone a fish. "What sort of magic is this?" Ramon asked.

"Looks like someone is trying to clean up this god forsaken realm," Treynor said with a laugh.

Soldiers appeared on the top of the battlements, aiming their weapons at the giants. Seeing the vampires next to the river and King Ambro at the tree line, Egon raised his hand for them to stand down and wait for further instructions.

The giants assumed a battle formation.

"What do you want here?" Egon called out.

"We are searching for the missing villagers," Treynor responded.

"Egon, is that you, old friend? What is this place? Why are you here?" Ambro asked, stepping out of the darkness, while avoiding the light.

"It is our new home, the way the realm used to be before you had the giants turn it dark. Since they are here, have them remove the curse they plagued us with."

Ambro's face grew red with pent up fury. "Are you insane? The light would kill us."

Avis joined Egon and pointed down at the vampires standing in the light. "Look at them Ambro. It's not hurting them. It hasn't hurt any of us. But the darkness is killing everything. Look around you. Nothing grows. Everything is dead." He yelled.

"We have to depend on the other realms for everything and we no longer have anything to trade," Avis accused.

Avis turned to Treynor. "Can you remove the darkness spell?"

Treynor frowned. He respected what Avis and Egon were doing. "I cannot. Our leader cast the spell. If it can be undone, it will have to be done by him."

Ambro stepped closer to Treynor. "Stop. This is my kingdom. I forbid you to reverse the spell."

Treynor bent down. His giant face inches from Ambro. "You forbid me nothing foolish old man. Keep your half of the realm dark and I will ask about reversing the spell. We have found your villagers as you requested." He waved to the other giants. "Let's go home."

"You can't leave. You have to get them out of there."

Treynor turned to Egon and Avis. "Are you keeping anyone against their will?"

Egon laughed. "Of course not."

"There you go. Come on, let's leave them to their business."

They quickly left the dead forest.

Ambro stared up at Avis and Egon. He raised his hands high above his head. A dark cloud appeared and quickly grew.

"Don't try anything stupid old man," Egon warned. Ambro's army stood between the King and Egon, unsure as to what to do.

Egon raised his staff and pointed it at the cloud as it rose above the King's head. Lightening flashed inside the cloud, then burst open raining down on the startled King, drenching him instantly.

Avis and Egon burst out laughing, infuriating the King even more. Aris stifled a laugh. Oref glared at her and she quickly hid her smile.

The cloud continued to grow. The parched ground sucked up the water thirstily. "Do something." Ambro yelled at his army.

Aris looked at the men and women around her. "What can we do? It's only water. Look how eagerly the ground drinks it. This is good for us."

"Arrest her," Ambro yelled pointing at Aris.

She looked around at her friends in panic. "You can't be serious?"

Oref reached out to her and she vanished in a puff of smoke and quickly drifted up toward Avis and Egon.

Egon lowered his staff. "Let her pass. Anyone who wants to make their life here is welcome to join us. You are free to leave at any time."

Nearly one-half of the remaining army vanished and quickly floated over the wall. "Nooo!" Screamed Ambro. Stop them. Don't just stand there. Do something."

"Your magic is no match for ours old man. Take your subjects," he said sneering the word, "and go home. Until the time comes for you to agree to return this realm to the way it was before you cursed it, there is no place for you here." Avis threatened.

"Now go," yelled Egon, pointing his staff at Ambro.

"This isn't over. I will have my people back."

"Take what's left of your foolish people and go," Egon yelled.

"Avis, why are you doing this?" Oref asked his friend.

"My friend, if you could see how beautiful it is inside you would understand." Avis held out his hands. "Look how much healthier we are than you. The darkness is killing you."

He could see the truth of his words. He winked at Avis and turned away and vanished into the dark forest.

Egon raised his staff and extended the light twenty feet in all directions."

Ambro groaned loudly and vanished with his foolish followers.

The trees and earth welcomed the warmth of the light. Egon and Avis quickly joined the bewildered vampires. Aris and Ramon were standing together looking around in awe. The others wandered around the courtyard in disbelief.

Aris spotted Avis and ran to him, hugging him warmly. "This is amazing. Is this really what our realm used to look like?"

Avis returned the hug. "Yes. And everything we said is true."

"We are dying?"

"Not if you live here. Your body will heal. You will be stronger than ever before."

"Why would he do this?"

"Fear, and control."

"Gather around everyone," Egon said. "Welcome to Opaque." He pointed up at the star above them, glowing near the top of the fortress. "United we can rebuild this land and thrive once again."

The vampires looked around at the witches, werewolves, and sorcerers fearfully. "Don't be afraid," Avis reassured them. We work and live together and continue to grow stronger."

"Alone we perish," Egon said. "If you can't live alongside all the members of this realm, you are free to go."

No one left.

"We have lodgings for everyone. Find a place to live. We have supplies. Avis will show you where everything is. Dinner is in an hour and we will explain everything to you then."

Ambro and his remaining army fled through the dead forest and returned to the castle. Ambro took human form on the castle steps, quickly followed by his faithful.

"I want to reward your loyalty by inviting every one of you to move into the castle. I don't know what spell Egon has cast but we will get to the bottom of this."

Rianna, a young vampire stepped forward. "Thank you, your majesty. I would be honored to accept your generous offer."

"You are most welcome. It is important that we all stand together."

"Your majesty," Rianna said, "What if they are right? What if we are dying?"

"That's absurd. Do we look like we're dying?"

"No, we don't."

"Please, everyone, move to the castle so we can formulate a plan."

Unsure, the vampires disbursed, returning to their homes to retrieve their belongings to move to the castle.

Oref gathered his wife and two young daughters, along with most of their belongings and quickly left their small house.

They kept to the shadows, silently making their way to the deserted town. The dead forest creaked and groaned in the silence. Part of it was struggling to return to life. A small green bud had taken root in the lower branch of a once dead tree.

Belina, Oref's wife pulled her small daughters closer as she looked at the massive fortress. "Are you certain we are doing the right thing?"

"Absolutely. The kingdom is dying. This is a chance for us to thrive." Oref created a small ball of light to gain the attention from someone inside the fortress.

"Who's there?" asked the guard on the battlement wall.

Avis appeared next to him. "Come on inside," he said, rubbing his hands together to remove the spell protecting the fortress.

Oref hefted the bags containing their belongings on his shoulder as stairs formed at his feet. The stairs made their way to the top of the fortress.

Avis turned and smiled at Egon who had just joined them.

Oref and Belina took their daughter's hands and climbed up the stairs together. The steps disappeared as they made their way to the top of the fortress.

Egon and Avis gently took the hands of the two children and helped them on the narrow wooden platform built into the stone wall.

The children looked down at the ground far beneath their feet and gripped their hands tighter.

Egon took the children a few feet away to make room for Oref and Belina. Avis clapped Oref on the back and hugged Belina. "I'm glad you are here my friends. I promise, you won't be sorry.

King Ambro's dark castle was bursting with excitement as his army and their families moved into the castle. Ambro quickly sent off a missive to the giants regarding Mags and the rescue of his son.

As soon as Dak returned they would return the kingdom to normal, then he'd deal with the giants for the way they disrespected him.

Chapter Eleven

The Lies Unfold

The days and weeks passed in a blur of training, and getting to know Mags and Dak. Dak was unlike anyone she'd ever know before. He was kind, sweet, and overly protective of her; which she found endearing.

Dak and Sierra walked down the marble stairs, glittering like gold dust in the warm sunlight. Sierra linked her arm through his as they headed down the back path framed by delicate pink flowers, away from the castle.

They had grown closer during the weeks they had spent training together.

Dak shifted the woven picnic basket on his arm while pulling Sierra closer with his other arm.

Sierra smiled up at him warmly. "So, what's in the basket?"

"It's a surprise," he teased.

"I hope it's good. I'm famished. Practicing magic works up an appetite."

"Iera helped me pack it, so I'm sure we're in for a surprise."

"I hope the surprise is one of her magical tarts."

Dak led Sierra off the shell path, across the thick blue green grass to a shaded spot next to the river, beneath a tree overflowing with pink blossoms. He released her arm and set the basket on the lush grass.

He pulled a soft red blanket out of the basket and laid it out smoothly across the grass. He took Sierra's hand and helped her onto the blanket and sat down beside her.

"You did really great today. Don't be afraid of your magic."

Sierra blushed lowering her head. "This is so new to me. I have no idea how to control it."

Dak put his finger beneath her chin and raised her face to look at him. "Stop trying to control it. Relax and let it work through you."

Sierra met his gaze and smiled shyly. "I'll try," she whispered.

Dak moved closer and covered her mouth with his, kissing her gently.

Sierra closed her eyes, returning his kiss.

Reluctantly, Dak pulled away, running his finger across her bottom lip. "I've wanted to do that ever since you stole my roast beef."

Sierra laughed and Dak kissed her again. Breaking the spell, he pulled away and opened the lid on the wicker basket. He pulled out a plate piled with fresh roast beef and potatoes.

Next were Iera's special tarts, covered in strawberries. He uncovered a plate of fresh fruit, and steamed vegetables. They both filled their plates. Sierra savored a piece of roast beef while Dak poured her a glass of honeysuckle nectar.

Dak laughed, "Mags would be horrified to see you tear into that roast beef."

"Mags has seen me eat beef on multiple occasions."

"You scared her for life, telling her that she used to eat birds."

Sierra laughed, "I thought she handled it very well.

"She's a very wise and good person." Dak said solemnly.

Sierra popped a tart in her mouth, savoring the strawberry, banana pudding flavor. She studied Dak's handsome face. She hated to see him look so sad. "You're thinking about your father again," she said.

"He lied to me about everything. What kind of a father does that?"

"I don't know," she said softly.

"Don't you miss your family? They must be worried about you."

Sierra frowned. "They were away on a trip when I left. I didn't mean to be gone so long. They must be worried"

Dak took both of her hands in his, "I'm sorry if I made you sad." He pulled her into his arms, resting her head against his chest. "I'll go to your home with you."

Sierra looked up at him, pulling him down to her and kissed him softly.

Dak stroked her cheek with his fingers and softly whispered against her lip, "I'd do anything for you."

Sierra pulled away from him and looked deep into his eyes. She could see his love for her reflected in their dark depths.

"I feel the same," she replied and kissed him again. Later, lying in his arms in the warm sun, she asked, "Do you want to return home?"

"My home is wherever you are. There is nothing there for me."

"What if you lose your magic if you go home with me? What if we can't get it back?"

Dak smiled, kissing the tip of her nose. "We'll make sure Mags can get us back, and I can survive without magic."

"You have an answer for everything."

"You should talk to Mags about returning to your home. Your family must be worried."

"I'll talk to her after training."

⚜ ⚜ ⚜

Sierra took Dak's advice and let the magic work through her. To her delight, she recreated the protective bubble around her with ease.

Dak created an unusual bouquet of flowers and gave them to Mags.

Mags smiled, accepting the kind gesture. She noticed the way Dak and Sierra looked at one another. She was delighted for the two of them. She knew that Sierra wasn't happy at home, and Dak's father had lied to him his entire life. They deserved to be happy.

"Mags," Sierra said.

"Yes dear. Is something wrong?"

"I need to let my family know that I'm all right. I shouldn't have stayed away for so long."

"It has been even longer in your world. Time moves more slowly here," Mags said.

Sierra's eyes widen in surprise. "How much slower? They must be frantic," she said.

"I'm sorry. I should have insisted that you return sooner," Mags said.

"Can you make sure that we can return?" Dak asked.

Mags was surprised that Dak wanted to go with her. "Yes," she said, smiling. "I will put a spell on you to protect you from the sun's rays."

"Can you send us now? I have to let them know that I'm okay."

"Of course." Mags raised her hand above Dak's head and cast the spells to make certain that the sun wouldn't hurt him.

"The spell will be easier for you since you are returning to your world. It will take the magic you both possess to make it work. I will send you home and if your magic works in your realm you will have to picture yourself back here, and say *alos gotto*. You must picture the place you want to return to in your mind. The spell only works between places you are familiar with."

"Are you sure it will work?" Sierra asked.

Mags took her hand in hers and kissed her warmly on the cheek. "Yes dear. Make things right with your mother. She loves you."

A single tear rolled down Sierra's smooth cheek. She quickly wiped it away. "I know she does. I will make things right."

"I'm trusting you to take care of her Dak," Mags said.

"I give you my word."

Mags raised her slender arms high above her head. "Alas gotto," she whispered softly, picturing Sierra's bedroom in her mind.

Dak linked his fingers with Sierra's as they grew faint and vanished from sight.

Mags crossed her arms over her chest. "Good luck," she whispered.

Sierra and Dak appeared in her bedroom. Dak looked around taking in everything. There were so many things he'd never seen before, it was hard to absorb it all in. "Where are we?" he asked.

"My bedroom."

"This is awesome," he said, letting go of her hand. He moved around her room, studying the pictures of her and her friends stuck on the brightly colored wall. He picked up a picture of her and her family in a silver frame sitting on her cluttered desk.

He picked up her cell phone and shook it. "What's this?"

"My phone," she said absently, taking a deep breath as she opened her bedroom door.

A woman in her forties with short blond hair stopped in the doorway in shock.

Sierra exhaled softly. "Hi mom."

Erin covered her mouth with her hand, then crossed the room pulling Sierra into her arms and kissed her softly on the cheek. "Where have you been? It's been months. We thought you were dead," she said, tears streaming down her face.

Sierra hugged her mother tighter. "I'm sorry mom. I didn't mean to be gone for so long, but I can explain."

"Explain? You disappeared while we were at my mothers. Not one word, and you even left your phone behind. We thought you'd been kidnapped or worse," she said. Noticing Dak standing uncomfortably next to the bed, she asked angrily, "Who is your friend? Is he the reason you ran away?"

"I didn't run away," Sierra said, trying to explain.

Dak crossed the room and extended his hand, "Dakota Rambolet, ma'am."

Sierra mouthed "Dakota?"

"I'm Erin, Sierra's mother," Erin said coldly, before turning back to Sierra, "Where have you been? I deserve an explanation."

Sierra chewed nervously on her lower lip. "You might want to sit own. It's a long story."

Erin clasped Sierra's hand in hers. "Are you in trouble?"

"No Mom, it's nothing like that." Sierra pulled Erin across the room and pulled her down on the bed next to her. She took a deep breath and her adventure poured out of her. She told her about Mags and learning magic. She told her about the people in the different realms.

She left out that Dak's father was the reason why they fled to their world.

Erin looked back and forth between Sierra and Dak. "Are you on drugs?"

Sierra stared at Erin in disbelief. "No. I came home because I didn't want you to worry."

"Too late for that, isn't it?"

"This was a mistake. Let's go Dak. She never listens to me. She thinks she can plan out my entire life without asking me even once what I want." Sierra jumped to her feet in anger and frustration.

Dak stood next to the bed with his mouth slightly open in surprise, then shut it abruptly, not wanting Erin to see his fangs.

Erin rose to her feet and seized Sierra by the wrist, and turned her around to face her. "What are you talking about? Why are you so angry with me?"

Sierra tried to jerk her hand free, but Erin held her tightly.

Dak could see the fury in Sierra's smoldering blue eyes. He found his voice and said, "Sierra's telling you the truth. I'm not from your world."

Erin turned and glared at him. "You need to go home young man. This is between me and my daughter."

"I won't leave without Sierra."

"She's not going anywhere with you."

Dak sighed. This wasn't going well. He didn't know if his magic would work, but he had to give it a try. He vanished in a puff of smoke, flew next to Sierra and reappeared.

Erin released Sierra's hand with a gasp and took a step backward. "What are you?" She stammered, noticing his fangs.

Feigning ignorance, he stared at Erin without saying anything.

"Are you the reason my daughter left?"

"No, I met her after she left. We came back because she didn't want you to worry. She loves you very much, but you need to listen to her. Really listen to her and get to know who your daughter really is."

Sierra smiled in gratitude, and looked at her mother.

"I'll leave the two of you alone to talk. I'll be somewhere on the other side of that door." Dak said, hurrying from the room, shutting the door behind him.

He looked around the hallway and had no idea where he should go."

Erin and Sierra stared at each other in silence. Erin crossed her arms defensively across her breast. "I'm sorry. I didn't realize I was planning your life."

Sierra sat down on her bed, pulling her knees up to her chest. She wrapped her arms around her legs. "Mom, you've picked the college you want me to attend, what I'm going to major in, where I'll work after graduation…"

"I didn't realize. I just want what's best for you."

"I know that, but I need to make these decisions for myself and for now, all of that's on hold. I'm going back to Bresslewood to discover how I can do magic."

"You can't. Your life is here."

"It isn't now. This is something I have to do."

Erin wrapped her arms around Sierra. "I don't want to lose you. I love you."

"You won't lose me. I'll always come home."

Erin hugged Sierra tightly, holding her like she wouldn't let go.

Dak stood outside the door shifting from one foot to the other.

Fifteen-year-old, Adam Winslow jogged up the stairs and stopped at the top. When he saw Dak standing outside Sierra's bedroom. His brows drew together as he studied Dak's strange dark clothing. His Goth look was a little creepy and not Sierra's type at all. "Hey dude, what's up? Is Sierra home?"

Dak looked at the teenage boy and wondered what language he was speaking. "I'm waiting for Sierra."

"I can see that bro. She run off with you? Bet mom flipped out," he laughed.

Dak had no idea what he was saying."

"Dude, you sure are quiet."

"Sometimes that is a good thing," Dak said, wishing the young man would stop talking.

"Yeah, whatever. So, you just hanging out in the hall or are you listening at the door?"

"I'm giving them privacy so they can talk."

So, where's Sisi been? She run off with you?"

"Sisi?"

"Sierra, my sister. Keep up, geesh."

"I assure you, that she didn't run away."

Erin hugged Sierra again and wiped the tears off her smooth cheeks. "I'm so sorry that I forgot that it was your life and let you make your own choices. Please forgive me."

Sierra threw her arms around Erin's neck. "I love you. I have to see where this leads me. I hope you understand."

"I do, but I don't like it."

Adam brushed past Dak and stormed inside Sierra's room. "Hey sis, who's the quiet dude lurking outside your door?" Adam asked, taking in his mom's and sisters tear stained faces. "Is everything all right?" he asked, suddenly worried.

Erin and Sierra exchanged looks and laughed. "Everything is fine. Your sister has a lot to tell you." Erin said.

Erin linked her arm through Dak's and led him downstairs to the kitchen. She poured them each a soft drink over ice and carried them to the kitchen table, setting a glass in front of Dak.

Dak had never been so nervous in his life. He took a sip of the strange brown drink. Its brisk taste burned his tongue and the back of his throat.

"This place you come from, is it safe?" Erin asked. "Is my daughter safe there?"

"Yes ma'am."

"What is this world of magic like?"

"Most of it is filled with beauty and wonders, but that's how Sierra described your world."

"I can't believe our cat is a queen," she laughed. "Sierra said she would ask if we can visit."

"I'm sure Lady Mags would love to have you."

She exhaled softly. "This is a lot to process."

He was spared a reply by Sierra and Adam entering the kitchen, laughing.

"Mom, Sierra said we can come for a visit. Isn't that cool? I wonder if I can do magic?"

"Lord I hope not," laughed Erin.

"Show us some magic," Adam said, ignoring his mother.

'I don't know if it works here, but I'll try."

Sierra closed her eyes and concentrated. A small white cloud appeared above Adams head. A light snow fell from the cloud.

Stunned, Adam poked his finger inside the cloud. It was cool and damp. "Awesome sis," he said giving her a high five.

Sierra bowed slightly from the waist. "Thank you," she said smiling.

Erin stared in awe at the cloud then at Sierra "That's amazing."

"Can I keep it?" Adam asked, poking the little cloud.

Sierra laughed, waved her hand, making the cloud vanish. "I'd like to show Dak around town. We won't be gone long."

Erin smiled, hating to see her leave, even for a short time, and said, "Have fun. I'll have dinner ready when you get back."

Sierra jumped to her feet, grabbed Dak by the hand and the car keys with the other hand. They were out the front door before Erin could blink.

The sun was setting between the mountains. The air was cool and crisp. Dak pulled her to a stop as he looked around the middle-class neighborhood lined with cars. He took a deep breath and exhaled. "The air is so clean."

Sierra pulled on his hand getting him moving. She clicked unlock on the fob and opened the door to her compact car, nearly shoving him inside.

She climbed in the car and reached across to fasten his seat belt.

"I hope Mags' spell against the sun last forever," he said softly.

Sierra smiled and started the car and pulled away from the curb.

Dak gripped the dashboard. "What is this thing?"

"It's called a car. We use it to get around."

"Is it safe?"

"Most of the time. Relax." She drove around the small Midwestern town, pointing out where she went to school, where she played tennis, where she hung out with her friends.

She was sitting at a red light when her friend Bree pulled up next to her. She honked and rolled down her window.

Sierra rolled down the window next to Dak and smiled at Bree.

"Where in the hell have you been?"

"It's a long story. Meet me at the tennis court and I'll try to explain."

Sierra pulled her car behind Bree's red mustang. She took a deep breath and climbed out of the car.

Dak grabbed her wrist. "Do you think it's wise to tell her?"

"No, probably not. I'll be right back."

Bree nearly jumped out of her car and tackled Sierra, twirling her around in a bear hug. "Where have you been?"

"I missed you too." Sierra laughed returning her hug. 'I've been staying with my grandparents. I needed some time to deal with the situation between my mom and me."

"Are things better?"

"Yes, she actually listened. I think we will be okay now."

"That's huge. I'm so happy for you."

"I know, right? I'm going to stay with my grandparents for a little longer so we won't screw up our fragile truce."

"Your mom cool with that?"

Sierra cocked her head to one side and smiled. "Actually, she is. She feels bad for not listening to me. I think we can fix this."

"That's awesome. Your mom is cool except for planning out your entire life for you," laughed Bree. "You better call me while you're gone. I was really worried about you. Your mom was worried too. You should have told somcone where you'd gone."

"I'm sorry. The cell service stinks and the storm knocked out the land line," she lied, taking Bree's hands in hers.

Bree peeked around Sierra. "Who's the hottie in the car?"

Sierra blushed, smiling. "He's a friend."

"Nice looking friend. No wonder you didn't call me. You were too busy. I forgive you," she teased, kissing Sierra on the cheek.

"You should come over later. I'll only be here a couple of days. My grandma isn't feeling well, so I'm helping to take care of her."

Bree released Sierra's hands. "I'll see you later then." She waved at Dak and hurried to her car. With one last wave, she drove away. Sierra smiled and returned the wave while she climbed into her car.

"She is your friend?" Dak asked.

"My best friend. You will get to meet her later."

"Your world is very different. Don't you miss it?"

"Of course, I do, but I feel drawn to your world."

Dak took her hand in his and kissed her fingers. "Or drawn to me?"

Sierra blushed, and avoided his piercing gaze. "That too," she laughed. "But seriously. I'm drawn to something there. I want to know what it is and why I possess magic."

Dak squeezed her hand. "I'm glad you came to our realm."

She squeezed his hand in return. "I'm glad too." She put in her favorite CD. "I want to show you around my town."

Dak jumped in surprise and looked around for the location of the music. "What is that?" he asked, bewildered."

Sierra laughed. "Music."

"I know what music is and that's not music."

"Don't make fun of my music," she teased.

Dak studied her face, and frowned. "This is really music?"

"Of course it is."

"You find this relaxing?"

"Sometimes. I mostly just enjoy it."

"Interesting."

Sierra laughed. She showed him her favorite spot at the lake, where the moon reflected in the dark cool depths. She showed him her high school, even though he had no idea what it was. The parents in his realm taught their children. He liked the idea of school.

Dak was amazed and overwhelmed by all the wonders of Sierra's world. It scared him that she'd return to it sooner than later.

Sierra smiled at him reassuringly as if reading his mind. "I'm not going anywhere."

— · — · —   — · — · —   — · — · —

Bree was late for dinner and came in like a whirlwind monopolizing the conversation. Adam practically drooled over every word she uttered.

Dak watched him in silent amusement. The boy was in over his head with Bree. He looked around the table at Sierra's family, glad that Erin had told her dad, James, about everything while they were gone.

James winked at him and Dak realized that this is what a family was supposed to be. Sierra would be shocked by his realm and his father.

After dinner they gathered in the living room to watch a movie. Dak was enthralled with the magic of Sierra's world. He sat on the edge of his seat enthralled with the story that played out on the television. He couldn't believe how real it was. This was a very different type of magic. He was sad when the movie ended.

Sierra walked Bree out to her car when the movie was over. "Don't forget to call me."

"I won't. I'm sorry I worried you."

"Tell that boyfriend of yours, if he hurts you, I'll cut off his favorite body part."

Sierra laughed. "I will not. It will scare him away."

"You really like him?"

"I do," she replied taking Bree's hands in hers. "I've never known anyone like him."

"Doesn't hurt that he's cute as hell." Bree laughed, squeezing her hands. She kissed Sierra on the cheek and added, "Don't stay away too long. I miss you like crazy."

Tears stung Sierra's eyes. "I won't. I promise."

"Okay then. I'll talk to you soon."

Sierra watched her drive away, wiping the unshed tears from her eyes. Sierra opened the door, startling her father who was deep in conversation with Dak. Her gaze met Dak's. She raised her brow in question.

Dak smiled back in reply.

James turned around, pulling Sierra next to him, encircling her waist with his arm. He kissed the top of her head lovingly. "Your young man has promised that the two of you will come back soon."

"Oh, he did," she said, punching Dak in the arm.

James pulled Sierra into his arms, hugging her tightly. "Please come back to us. My heart can't take it, if you don't," he cried, his tears dropping on her cheek.

Sierra reached up and brushed them away. "I promise Daddy."

"I understand you're being compelled to do this, but this is your home."

Dak felt his heart sink. Sierra's family couldn't bear it if she didn't return home. How could he ask her to stay?

And you better come back with her." James said to Dak.

Sierra reached out and took Dak's hand. "He will if I have to drag him back," she teased.

"I would be delighted to return to your lovely world. I can only imagine that there are many wonders for me to see."

"It could take a lifetime," James said softly.

Chapter Twelve

Home

Dak softly shut the door to Sierra's bedroom behind him. He took a deep breath before turning around to face her. "I'd understand if you want to stay here with your family."

Fighting back tears, Sierra said, "Of course I want to stay with them. Three days wasn't long enough."

Dak felt as if he'd just been punched in the stomach.

"But I want to be with you too. I love you," she continued softly.

Dak stared at her briefly before pulling her roughly into his arms kissing her in desperation. "Don't ever scare me like that," he said against her lips before kissing her again.

Sierra clung to Dak, returning his kiss, caressing his cheek softly with the back of her fingers. "After we complete our training and see if we can discover the source of my magic, can we come back here for a while?"

Dak brushed his lips softly against hers. "I'll go wherever you are."

Sierra smiled, blushing. "We better get some rest, we have to return tomorrow," she said, pulling away.

Dak softly brushed his lips against hers and turned away. "Sleep well."

Alone in her room, Sierra dropped down on her bed. She pulled her favorite teddy bear into her arms and hugged it tightly. She wiped a single tear from her cheek. It was going to be so hard to leave tomorrow.

Morning came too soon. Sierra located Dak in the kitchen learning how to heat water in the microwave. He heard Sierra plop down in a bar stool at the long marble bar, and turned and smiled at her.

Sierra returned his smile. "Good morning." She said.

"Good morning," Dak and Erin said together.

"The magic of your world is amazing." Dak said, looking back at the microwave.

Erin laughed and shrugged. "It's not magic. It's a microwave. It's technology," she said.

"Like television?" he asked.

"Just like television."

"Technology is like magic."

Sierra opened her mouth, then shut it. She smiled at Dak. "I guess it is like magic."

The microwave buzzed. Erin handed Dak a pot holder and he carefully removed the cup and set it on the counter.

"What's the water for?" Sierra asked.

"For?" Dak asked in confusion.

"Why are you heating up water?"

Dak laughed. "No reason. I like the microwave." He shrugged.

Erin put four plates on the counter just as Adam entered the kitchen. She put plates filled with eggs, bacon and toast down on the bar. She glanced at Sierra and held back tears. She didn't want her to leave again.

Sierra saw her unshed tears and reached across the bar and grabbed her hand and squeezed it, mouthing, "I love you."

Erin squeezed her hand. "I love you too," she whispered.

Adam quickly filled his plate and sat down next to Sierra. "So, you're leaving again?"

Sierra punched him playfully in the arm. "Sorry. I'll be back before you know it."

"Great. I was hoping to get your room," he teased.

Sierra playfully gripped him by the arms. "Touch one thing in my room and I'll sell your PlayStation."

"You wouldn't?" he said, feigning horror.

"I would." She laughed.

Dak watched them in confusion.

Erin laughed. "Eat your breakfast. It's getting cold."

Hating to prolong the goodbyes, Sierra hugged her mother and brother goodbye repeatedly. "Please tell Dad bye for me again."

"He hated that he had to go to work."

"I know. He told me last night. I will see you again soon."

"How do you get back?" Adam asked.

"Mags gave me the spell. All I have to do is picture where I want to go in my mind and recite the spell. If it works, we will leave here and reappear there."

"Awesome, you teleport" Adam said excitedly.

Sierra chewed on her lip, "I guess we do," Sierra hugged Adam and Erin one last time.

"Can you go anywhere like that?"

"No, just back to Bresslewood for now. I still have a lot to learn in the magic department," she said.

Dak shook Adam's hand and hugged Erin.

Hugging her brother and mother one last time, Sierra took Dak's hands, closed her eyes and pictured her and Dak at the clearing where they had the picnic.

Adam and Erin watched in amazement as Sierra and Dak vanished in front of them.

They reappeared in the clearing. Dak looked around and smiled. "You did it."

"We did it." She said, smiling.

Dak pulled her into his arms and kissed her softly.

She looked out across the land. A sea of flowers of multiple colors grew as far as she could see. The cool breeze carried their sweet fragrance to them.

Sierra frowned slightly. A dust storm appeared in the distance. It was moving fast, too fast for an ordinary storm. "Look," she said, pointing at the dark cloud.

Dak shielded his eyes from the setting sun with his hand. "What do you think that is?"

"I don't know."

"Wait here." Dak said, turning into a shadow. He quickly covered the distance to the mysterious sand storm. Keeping his distance, he hovered several yards away, watching the giants make their way toward Bresslewood.

Without hesitation, he hurried back to Sierra. "The giants are heading this way. I need to warn the queen." He quickly kissed Sierra before disappearing again.

Sierra broke into a run, down the hill toward the castle.

Dak reappeared in front of Mags sitting at a small table in the throne room.

Mags jumped to her feet, startled by his sudden appearance. "I'm sorry. I didn't mean to frighten you my lady."

"Whatever is the matter? Is Sierra all right?" she asked seeing how worried he was.

"The giants are marching toward the castle."

Without hesitation, Mags signaled the alarm, and raced from the throne room toward the castle doors.

Dak raced after her.

Outside on the luscious blue green lawn, her army was already assembling. Slade and Rhys quickly flanked her side.

Dak took a position on her right. Sierra, out of breath, joined him.

Mags smiled in appreciation at them. She waved her hand and a thin delicate yet impenetrable chain of white armor appeared on Sierra. Dak's was black.

They stood on the crest of the hill, Mags army, dressed in white armor, watching, waiting expectantly. The giants approached from the right, and a dark cloud appeared on the right at their side.

"Father," Dak whispered.

Sierra linked her fingers with Dak's. He smiled sadly at her. He felt sick inside. "I'm okay." He assured her.

The giants were led by a smaller, female giant.

Mags raised her hands creating a spell to stop the giants. She is startled when it didn't work. She used the same spell on the shadowy vampires heading toward them. They are slowed, like they were moving through quicksand. "Something is blocking my spell." Mags said.

Sierra watched the approaching army of giants in fear. She raised her hand and concentrated. A large dark cloud appeared above the giants and cloud of vampires.

It quickly engulfed them. Lightening flashed in the cloud, striking the giants, knocking several of them to their knees.

The lady giant put her hand up to ward off the lightening and was surprised when the lightning bolt struck her hand, knocking her backward. She glanced across the valley toward Mags with hatred.

Dak faced the cloud of vampires and giants and sent a wave of fire toward them. The two groups retreated, trying to avoid the flames. The giants weren't so lucky. Several of them were on fire.

The vampires rose above the flames and headed across the field toward the castle.

Mags' army moved to intercept them.

Dak turned into smoke and took his place in front of Mags' army.

Sierra swallowed her fear for Dak and sent a wave of rocks to pelt the intruders.

The lady giant sent dozens of swords hurling at Mags. Sierra quickly put up a shield to protect them and sent the swords hurling back at the giants, followed by a burning stinging rain.

The stinging rain forced the vampires to take shape.

Ambro stopped short when he saw Dak leading Mags' army. He put up his hand for his army to wait. He looked at his son. The seconds ticked by.

Dak met his stare, glaring at Ambro in disappointment. He raised his hand, motioning the army forward.

Together, the army lifted their hands, creating a sonic boom that deafened both armies. Deaf and on fire, the giants surged forward in anger, slowing the advancement of Mags' army.

The lady giant cast a spell to protect the front of her army and sent a wave of water toward Mags and her army.

Dak reacted quickly, with a wave of his hand, the water split into four sections and went around the army.

Sierra and Mags froze the wall of water heading toward them. The water fell harmlessly to the ground.

Mags' soldiers drew their swords and raced toward the giants.

Dak cast a spell, freezing Ambro's army in place. Mag's soldiers darted around the giants protected by the lady giants' spell and attacked the remaining giants.

As their swords tore through them, they exploded in a whirlwind of leaves and twigs. The soldiers were surrounded by swirling leaves as they forged their way through the battlefield, reducing the giant's army to a pile of debris.

They looked back over the battlefield filled with mountains of leave and debris, at the remaining giant army advancing toward Mags.

To their amazement, the leaves and twigs swirled around them and begin to take shape and reform into giants. The exhausted knights raised their heavy swords and sliced through the newly formed giants. The swords have no effect this time.

"Retreat," Rhys called out. The giants ignored the men at their feet.

The giants quickly made their way toward Dak and the immobile vampires, who were slowly breaking free from Dak's spell.

Caught off guard by the sudden appearance of the giants, Dak's spell is broken. A yell went up among the vampires and they vanished into shadows and surged forward toward the castle.

Dak groaned in horror and quickly followed them, with the giants right behind him.

Sierra linked her fingers with Mags, grasping her hand tightly and closed her eyes. Taking a deep breathe they sent a wave of energy out over the approaching armies. The energy wave transformed the vampires back into their human form mid-flight, including Dak, who ended up face down in the grass, in the middle of his father's army.

He jumped to his feet and broke into a run, fighting off several of his former friends on his way up the hill, where he came face to face with his father.

Dak didn't hesitate, and shoved Ambro aside and continued up the hill.

The reformed giants, under Sierra's control overtook the vampires, subduing them easily since they couldn't transform. They surrounded them as the energy field imprisoned them.

Dak reached the approaching giants and drew his sword.

Mags cast a spell at the giants, but the protective spell rendered it harmless. Mags turned to Sierra, "I don't understand why my magic doesn't work."

Sierra squeezed her hand reassuringly. "It's okay. We are defeating them. I'm drawing on your strength for my spells."

"I can feel it. Your magic is very strong. By the way, welcome back," she laughed.

"Glad we were here to help."

"I don't think we would have defeated them without you."

The lady giant and her six followers reached the castle steps, protected by another spell.

Mags studied the giantess closely. Something about her was very familiar. "You should surrender." Mags cried out. "Your army has been defeated."

The lady giant's head turned around, stunned to see her army keeping the vampires from assisting them in the battle. Fuming, she glared at Mags. "It isn't over yet." She yelled, taking a step forward.

Under her breath, Sierra muttered "Beniti asla insanti." A thin mist appeared out of nowhere coating everything in a fine sheen. The magic spell protecting the giants dissolved, as did the magic holding them together. The giants shrunk to their natural size, looking small and helpless at the foot of the stairs.

Mags quickly glanced at Sierra in awe and wonder, before descending the steps to face her attackers. Face to face with their leader, she stepped backward in shock, her hands covering her heart.

"Mavis?" she said in shock.

"Hello sister. This is far from over."

"How? Why? I thought you were dead," she asked, hurt and confused.

"Sorry to disappoint you," she said before disappearing in a cloud of red smoke.

Sierra tried to stop her, but she was too late. Mavis had escaped, leaving her people behind. The former giants looked at Mags in fear.

Dak stopped next to her and stared out over the meadow. Gone were the flowers of every color. They were trampled and broken, lying in the mud.

His gaze drifted to the giants surrounding his friends and family and felt sick. "What about them?" he asked.

Sierra broke the spell holding the giants together and they dissolved into a pile of twigs and leaves. Her spell continued to hold the vampires in their human form.

Surrounded by her army, Mags smiled sadly at Dak. "Bring all the prisoners to my chambers." She turned and gracefully glided up the stairs, disappearing inside the castle. Alone, she leaned against the wall, fighting back tears. Her sister, alive and attacking her, why?

Wiping the tears from her cheeks, she continued to her chambers, taking her seat on her throne. She took a deep breath and tried to pull herself together.

She looked calm and collected when Dak, Sierra and her army entered her chambers escorting the prisoners.

Dak and Sierra took up a position beside Mags' throne, with Rhys and Slade on each side of them. Dak avoided looking at his people. He concentrated his gaze on the former giants.

Sierra's spell kept the vampires under control.

Mags instructed her army to move the former giants forward. She studied the men who refused to meet her gaze. "It's obvious that Mavis' magic transformed you into giants. Where are the real giants?"

The men looked nervously around at each other. None of them spoke up.

"You can tell me or I can use a spell to force you to tell me. It's up to you."

Treynor stepped forward. Marcus tried to put his hand on his shoulder, threateningly. Treynor shrugged it off. "Why protect her? She ran and left us here. Mavis has them locked in the dungeon beneath the town hall."

"How? It would have to be enormous to hold them."

"She put a spell on them. They are the size of small animal."

"What did Mavis hope to accomplish here?"

"She wanted your throne. You must have really pissed her off. She really hates you." He said smugly.

"Shut up," yelled Marcus.

Mags raised her hand and silenced him. His words stung. Why would Mavis hate her? "Thank you," she said softly, lost in thought. "Please take them to the dungeon. I will decide what to do with them later. Please bring King Ambro forward."

Sierra released him from the binding spell, but continued to hold his form so he couldn't transform.

Ambro moved forward reluctantly. His gaze burned through Dak.

Dak's gaze swept over his father in disappointment.

"Are you going to just stand there?" Ambro yelled at Dak.

"What would you have me do Father? You attacked the kingdom."

"We came to rescue you."

"From what?"

"I thought you were being held prisoner."

"You can see that I'm not."

"When you didn't return after the gates opened, what was I to think?"

"You could have come to see for yourself."

"And risk being captured?"

"You are being irrational father. When has Lady Mags done anything to make you believe such nonsense? You sent me here on a fool's errand."

"She treats our realm unfairly."

"How is that?"

"She knows we can't attend the meetings. The sun will destroy us."

"That's…."

"That's not quite true," interrupted Egon, accompanied by Avis, Collin and Vestry. Ambro tried to speak, but Egon silenced him. "Pardon my interruption Lady Mags," he said bowing to her.

"Welcome Master Egon. It has been a long time. It is a pleasure to see you again." Mags said.

"I'd like to introduce you to the council of the Opaque. Myself, Avis, Collin and Lady Vestry. We are the governing body of our realm and would like your blessing and your help."

"You have my blessing, and your timing is perfect. I will let your council decide what to do with your people that tried to invade my realm."

Ambro struggled to break free from Sierra's spell.

"You can't do this. I am his king."

"It is done. You are no longer a king." Mags said, dismissing him.

"Son, how can you stand there and let her do this to me?"

Dak shook his head sadly. "You did this to yourself father."

"How can I help you Master Egon?" Mags asked.

"Our realm is dying without the sun. I have restored it to a small part of the realm, but my magic can't undo the spell of eternal darkness."

"I will visit your realm to see if I can reverse the spell. Lord Ambro, you could help by telling us who cast the original spell."

"It appears to have been your sister," he answered in disgust.

"I see. Thank you. When I visit, I'd like to meet with your council if you have time."

"We always have time for you my lady. It will be an honor and privilege to sit down with you."

"Please take your people home. I will see you in a few days' time."

"Thank you, my lady," Egon said.

Sierra removed her binding spell, glanced at Dak briefly and watched the vampires shift to their shadowy form and leave Mags' chambers.

Dak felt sick inside. His father would never accept this.

"I want to thank everyone. We fought valiantly today, but I'm afraid it isn't over yet. Rest and stay alert. Our absence seems to have created much unrest. I will need all of your help to restore peace to the realms."

Her army bowed together and turned and marched from the room through the remaining army that filled the great hall and spilled out and down the stairs.

Rhys and Slade excused themselves to see to the prisoners.

Mags exhaled sharply and looked at Dak. "Are you alright?" she asked.

"Honestly, I don't know," he said softly.

Sierra moved to his side, taking his hand in hers.

Mags studied Sierra, she was amazed at the power the young girl possessed. Without her, they would have been defeated today. "You were amazing today. Both of you were. I don't know how to thank you. I must ask one more thing of you."

"I'm glad we were here to help," Sierra said. "What else can we do to help?"

Dak smiled. He liked the way she spoke for them as one.

"I could use your help in freeing the giants and returning them to normal. Then we will see if we can help the dark realm. I'm afraid my sister's magic has made my spells ineffectual."

"How did she do that, and why?" Sierra asked.

"I don't know, but I plan on finding out. I thought my sister was dead. I don't know what I did to make her hate me." She said softly.

"I may be able to answer that." Dak said. "Power. She wants what you have. I've lived with that jealousy my entire life."

Sierra hugged him, resting her head against his chest.

Chapter Thirteen

Freeing the Giants

Sierra stood alone on top of the hill overlooking the battlefield. A strange sadness threatened to overtake her. She closed her eyes and held her hands up, palms out in front of her.

A power grew inside her and exited through her fingertips. The twigs and leaves that the giants were created from swirled together and disappeared.

The crushed flowers pushed up through the trampled grass, mixed with mud. The grass forced the mud down and the flowers straightened and returned to their pre-battle form.

The meadow returned to normal. Iera flew next to Sierra and watched as her magic healed the scarred land. She fluttered next to Sierra's face and studied her clam relaxed features in awe.

Sierra turned and looked at Iera and lowered her hands self-consciously to her side.

"I'm sorry to disturb you my lady." Iera said nervously.

"No worries. Did you need me?"

"Lady Mags is ready to travel to the giant's realm. They are waiting for you at the castle gate."

"Thank you. Please let her know that I'm on my way."

"Yes ma'am," Iera replied, taking one last look at the restored meadow before flying away.

Sierra watched her tiny pink and purple wings flutter against the wind. She looked down at her khaki shorts and pink tee shirt, deciding she wasn't dressed for a rescue mission.

She closed her eyes and ran her hands down the length of her body and transformed her shorts into skin tight black leather pants. Her sandals turned into black leather boot with her pants tucked neatly inside.

Her pink tee shirt became a purple tunic covered by a thin sliver chainmail glittering with the magic that protected her. Her hair, flying freely in the breeze, pulled away from her face into a French braid to hang in a braid down her back.

Smiling at her transformation, she hurried down the hill, crossed the wooden bridge leading to the castle to join Mags and her army, already astride horses readied for battle.

She strode across the courtyard to join them.

Dak's eyes raked over her skin-tight clothing in appreciation and smiled lovingly at her.

Mag's brows drew together in awe. Sierra was transforming before them. Her magic and confidence was growing every day. She would soon be the most powerful sorcerer the realms had ever seen. She whispered a silent prayer that it wouldn't destroy her.

Sierra nodded to Mags. "Sorry I'm late." She stuck her foot in her horse's stirrup and effortlessly climbed astride the muscled white stallion, draped with a purple blanket.

Dak urged his black gelding forward, stopping inches away from Sierra. "I love the outfit," he whispered softly.

Sierra blushed and smiled, looking deep into his dark eyes, filled with love for her.

Mags urged her horse forward and her army followed in behind her.

Dak and Sierra rode side by side, trailing slightly behind. "I like the new look," Dak said, smiling.

"It's my going into battle look," she teased.

"It suits you."

Her eyes raked over his black fitted pants, black shirt, black boots, and a black cape. "You could use a dash of color," she said shrugging slightly.

"I'll see what I can do about that," he teased. "Any particular color?"

"Surprise me."

They reached the gate and passed through one by one, regrouping on the other side. Sierra drank in the fresh cool air, looking around at the green hills in the distance.

Mags urged her horse into a run and they raced across the lush empty field. They reached the edge of the deserted town. The tall buildings loomed silently in the distance.

They slowed their pace as they entered the town. The clip clop from the horse's hooves was the only sound in the deafening silence, echoing eerily through the town.

They scanned the vacant streets, but there wasn't any sign of life. "This place gives me the creeps," Sierra said, shivering.

Dak looked up at the imposing building, draped in silence and nodded in agreement.

Sierra did a double take at Dak and smiled.

Dak tugged teasingly on the hot pink scarf draped around his neck. "You like it?" he asked, grinning like a child.

"It's lovely," she replied, giving him a thumbs up.

Mags stopped in front of a large building, and dismounted. Her troops followed suit.

Dak and Sierra dismounted and followed them inside.

Mags and her troops quickly crossed the enormous room. The ceilings were over thirty feet tall. Sierra's home would fit inside the room over twenty times. Sierra shivered. She wasn't sure if she wanted to meet the giants.

Dak linked his fingers with Sierra's squeezing her hand reassuringly. Sierra squeezed his hand in return and smiled nervously.

"How can a girl that held off an entire army be afraid of a few giants?" he whispered teasingly.

Sierra punched Dak in the arm smiling innocently.

Mags disappeared through a large door. Her army held back waiting for her.

Sierra hesitantly followed her through the door where Mags waited for them at the top of the stairs.

"The giants should be in the dungeon below. We will release them and take them upstairs before we try removing Mavis' spell." Mags said.

Sierra looked down at the cliff-like stairs and frowned uncertainly.

Mags smiled, raised her hands and created a smaller set of stairs down the middle of the oversized stairs.

"Nicely done my lady," Dak said, leading the way down the stairs.

Mags smiled and indicated with a wave of her hand for Sierra to precede her. It took them several minutes to reach the bottom.

Sierra exhaled sharply and looked around the dimly lit room filled with enormous cells occupied by animals nearly as tall as Dak. They appeared to turn all at once and glared at them. A strange growl or roar filled the room as they rushed the door to their cells, eager to be released.

Mags raised her hands and released the locks on the doors. They crashed to the stone floor with a metallic thud.

Sierra stepped back as they rushed past them and disappeared up the stairs. They tried to keep up, but it was useless. The animals possessed a catlike quickness.

Reaching the bottom of the steps, Sierra raised her hands and turned the simple wooden steps into an escalator.

Dak looked at the moving steps in wonder "Your magic is amazing," he said in awe.

Sierra shrugged and laughed. "Modern technology."

Mags laughed. "I wished I'd paid better attention to the marvels of your world."

Sierra took Dak by the hand and led him onto the moving escalator and stepped up behind him.

Mags easily joined them and they rode to the top, stepping off one by one.

Sierra removed the escalator and joined Mags and Dak in the great room filled with the colorful giant animals pacing nervously around the room. They excitedly rushed toward Mags.

Afraid for her safety, Sierra enclosed the three of them in a protective shield. The animals stopped, and circled the three of them.

Low growls filled the room growing louder as they became more and more agitated.

Mags tried repeatedly to reverse the spell Mavis cast on them. "I don't understand how Mavis has blocked my magic, but I have to find out before I face her again. I will have to travel to your realm Dak, and consult with Egon."

"I would love to see your realm," Sierra said excitedly.

Dak frowned, but remained silent. He wasn't eager to return to his home.

Sierra closed her eyes, raising her hand out in front of her. Her brows drawn together in confusion.

Dak raised his hands to assist her. He can feel the strange resistance too. Something is trying to stop them from removing the transformation spell.

The protective dome around them dissolved. The animals stopped moaning and growling. They suddenly looked afraid. Dak linked his fingers with Sierra, as Mags took her other hand.

She immediately felt the strange resistance to their magic. Sierra pulled power from a source she didn't know she possessed and ripped through the resistance.

A pale light that sparkled like glitter poured over the room covering everything and everyone. The animals were mesmerized by the warmth of the light as it washed over them, returning them to their former giant selves.

The giants towered over them, looking down in gratitude. One by one, they bowed in respect and gratitude to Mags, Sierra and Dak. "We can never thank you enough," said Aswaa, the giant leader. He studied the three before him with his dark blue eyes.

"We are in your debt. How can we ever repay you?"

"We may call upon you to help capture the one responsible for your imprisonment." Mags said.

"We will do that regardless. We will still remain in your debt."

"Do you know where she has gone?" Sheri, wife to Aswaa asked, bending down to study the three tiny humans before them.

I'm afraid not," Mags said, embarrassed by her sister's deeds. "We will find her. This will not go unpunished." Mags promised.

"Thank you, my lady. We will do what we can to discover her whereabouts."

"I must travel to the Dark Realm to consult with a wise sorcerer, then I will return and we will find Mavis."

"We shall await your return. With luck we will be able to locate her by the time you return." Aswaa stated.

"Is there anything you require before we go?"

"No, my lady. Thank you again for freeing us."

"Our pleasure. We will return soon." Mags promised.

Aswaa and Sheri stood to their full height and watched the tiny humans cross the room and exit through the enormous door.

Aswaa turned to his people. "Send the owls to every realm. I want this woman found."

Gariff nodded his dark head. "At once sir." He turned and went out the same door that Mags and her party had exited through moments before.

Gariff glanced at their departing figures riding away in the distance. He pulled a delicate flute from his pocket and blew into it. The sweetest notes filled the air. The tune was both hypnotic and peaceful. It seemed to calm the very air around him.

He could hear the sound of more than two dozen wings soaring through the sky.

A giant white owl landed on his shoulder, while the rest perched on the trees and buildings. "How can I be of service?" Narvan, the leader of the owls asked. His deep blue eyes filled with intelligence.

"You know of the woman that imprisoned us?"

"Yes. I apologize for not being able to assist you, but you made us vow not to show ourselves."

"There wasn't anything you could have done, but you can assist us now."

"In what way?"

"Travel to each realm and locate her. She will be punished for imprisoning us. Don't let anyone see you, and be very careful. She is very dangerous."

"We will find her." Narvan unfurled his milk white wings and flew into the air and disappeared. He hovered invisible in front of Gariff. "We shall return soon."

The other owls vanished from sight, their wings slicing through the air.

Chapter Fourteen

Traveling to the Dark Realm

Mags and her party reached the edge of the Giant Realm and passed through the gate reentering Mags' kingdom. They didn't slow down until they reached the gate between Bresslewood and the Dark Realm.

Mags stopped and turned her horse around and joined Sierra and Dak at the end of the line. She pulled up next to Dak, "I will understand if you would rather sit this one out."

"Thank you, but this is something I need to do. I owe it to my people."

Mags studied his handsome face. His dark eyes revealed nothing. "If you change your mind…"

"I won't," he assured her. Mags glanced at Sierra and back at Dak. "Very well." She turned her horse away and galloped back to the front of the line and disappeared through the gate.

Her army followed one by one until Dak and Sierra were alone. Sierra blocked his path with her horse. "You don't have to do this," she said, studying his pale face.

"Yes, I do. I need to redeem myself."

"For what? Too whom?" she cried. "You've done nothing to be redeemed for."

"I attacked Mags. That's why she fled to your world. This mess is all my fault," he said sadly.

"It's your father's fault. Besides, we wouldn't have met if none of this had happened," she reminded him.

Dak pulled his horse next to Sierra's and leaned across his horse and kissed her gently on the lips. "That would have been a travesty," he replied against her lips.

He pulled away grinning mischievously, a fire burning in his dark eyes. "Let's finish this," he said with determination.

He nudged his horse forward with his knees and vanished through the gate.

Sierra laughed and quickly urged her horse forward, following him through the gate. Everything she'd been told about the Dark Realm didn't prepare her for the complete desolation caused by decades without sunlight.

Everything was dead. The once tall and majestic trees were dry cracked pieces of wood held up by the hard-packed earth. Withered dead leaves hung desperately to the thin dead limbs.

It was utterly silent. No birds perched in the dead trees. No animals rustling in the tall dead grass. Not even the wind found its way through the lifeless world.

The darkness prevented Sierra from seeing very far into the distance. She hoped the entire realm wasn't like this. What a depressing place to grow up.

"Dak, can you lead us to the fortress that Egon told us about?" Mags asked.

Without looking at Sierra, afraid to see the pain on her face as she realized how truly horrible his home was, he replied, "Follow me," and urged his horse forward.

Sierra didn't try to keep up with him. She remained in her position behind Mag's army.

They traveled a couple of miles through the sad dead forest when the terrain began to change. At first, a couple of pale green leaves appeared on the trees. And dry patches of grass covered the ground, replacing the hard-packed dirt.

When they came to the top of a hill, you could see down into the valley below and it was teaming with life. The trees were in full bloom, surrounded by patches of flowers in the tall blue green grass.

The wind carried the sweet scent of the flowers and ripening fruit across the valley.

Sierra pulled her horse next to Dak. He was engrossed in the scene before him and didn't notice her presence at his side.

His eyes drank in the beauty that filled the valley. A crystal blue stream disappeared inside the enormous fortress that was flanked by a forest of trees.

A smile tugged at the corner of his mouth when he saw a red, yellow and orange parrot dart out of the trees followed by vampire and werewolf children laughing and screaming in delight.

He couldn't believe his eyes. Nothing like this had ever existed in his realm. He urged his horse down the hillside, eager to see more.

Startled by the approaching army, the children ran, disappearing inside the fortress.

Egon, Vestry, Collin and Avis appeared at the top of the wall that surrounded the fortress. A smile spread across their faces as they recognized their visitors.

The enormous gate slowly swung open to welcome them inside. Dak eagerly led the way across the wooden draw bridge. His eyes drank in the wonders around him.

As soon as Sierra was inside the fortress, the massive gate closed behind her.

Dak slid off his horse and Avis grabbed him in a tight bear hug. "Welcome to Opaque," he said excitedly. Dak looked across the orchard and fields teaming with life. "This is amazing," he cried excitedly.

Sierra stood silently to the side watching Dak with his friends.

Mags and her army dismounted. Egon quickly joined them. "Welcome my lady. We are honored by your visit," he said excitedly. "Please join us for refreshments in our council chamber," he continued, taking Mags by the arm.

Mags turned and waved for Dak and Sierra to join them.

"I will see to it that your people are served refreshments and given a tour of our lovely city if they so desire," Egon said.

"I'm sure they would love to see more of this marvelous city you created," Mags said.

Avis's eyes raked over Sierra in question as she took her place at Dak's side. They entered the council chambers. Egon, Avis, Collin and Vestry took their place at the table. Egon added a chair for Mags, to the surprise of the rest of the council.

Honored, Mags took her place at the table as Egon slid a green cloth wrapping something in its velvet softness, across the table. Mags opened the cloth to find a green stone nestled in its folds.

As soon as she picked it up the stone started to glow a soft green, filling the room with its light. The stone caused the amber star on the ceiling to pulsate.

The room grew quiet as the spectators filling the gallery stopped and stared at the spectacle of light filling the room.

Dak and Sierra took a protective stance behind Mags. The green light pulsated and joined the amber light above them, turning it to a soft yellow.

An awe filled the room as everyone marveled at what transpired. "Welcome to the council my lady," Egon said excitedly.

A cheer went up in the gallery. One by one, Mags was welcomed by the other council members. Outside the perimeter of light grew, absorbing more of the desolate landscape, giving it life.

The brittle trees drew strength from the light and earth, springing to life. Lush green grass spread across the once dead forest floor. A dry brittle tree absorbed the life-giving light and two small buds appeared it the upper most branches.

"Thank you, Egon. I am honored to be a part of your council," Mags said.

"It is we who are honored. To add your strength to our council gives new life to our realm."

"I am here to try and clear the darkness from your realm and to seek your council," Mags said.

The growing crowd cheered in excitement. A stern glare from Egon silenced them. "My council? How may I be of service?"

"I've just learned that my sister, Mavis is alive."

"That is wonderful news," interrupted Egon.

Mags' eyes grew sad and she lowered her head slightly.

"It isn't wonderful news?" he questioned in confusion.

"I'm extremely glad she's alive, but saddened by her actions. She imprisoned the giants and created new giants to take their place. With assistances from Ambro they are responsible for the attack on my kingdom."

"Other than the giants being fake, I know all of this my lady,"

"Yes, of course," she said twisting the green cloth between her fingers. "What you don't know is that somehow she's rendered my magic useless against hers."

"Oh my," he exclaimed.

"Can this spell be undone?"

Egon rose from his seat at the table, pacing back and forth across the room. His mind was racing. "It is an ancient spell, never used before, to my knowledge. Why would it be?" he rambled to himself. "Family against family. Sad times indeed."

Mags and Dak lowered their heads saddened by his words, and the implications to both of them.

"She used a blood spell to protect her against her family. You can't undo it, but you can invoke the same spell."

Mags stood appalled that she should have to protect herself from the sister she once loved and still loved. "She protected those around her. Can I do the same?" she asked rising to her feet. As she stood, the green stone fell to the stone floor with a clatter.

"Yes. It is possible."

Sierra bent down to retrieve the fallen stone. The instant her hand closed over the smooth dark stone it pulsed with a bright red light, filling the room with its brilliance.

Everyone turned and stared at her in surprise and shock. The warm light was filled with a life-giving force that was immediately felt by everyone in the realm. "I'm sorry," Sierra stammered trying to set the stone down on the council table.

"Stop," yelled Egon. "Don't put it down." Egon moved quickly to her side.

Dak moved closer, protectively putting his arm around her waist. The instant he touched her, the light turned from red to blue, back to red.

"What is this?" Egon whispered excitedly.

Outside the change in the realm was astonishing. The light completely dispelled the darkness. Life returned to the realm. What was once dead and dormant was now teaming with life.

Birds and animals appeared out of nothing, as did flowers, plants and streams. What was once dark and lifeless was now extraordinarily beautiful. The change in the people was nearly as alarming.

Dak's pale cheeks turned pink, then tan. If possible, he was more handsome than ever.

"Oh my," whispered Egon. "Where are you from my child?"

Sierra was suddenly afraid. She couldn't explain what has just happened. As she started to set the glowing stone on the table, it shot up to the star, glowing on the ceiling. Instead of joining the star, it took its place in the center, filling the room with its red glow.

Dak put his arm around her tighter. He didn't like the vibe emanating from everyone.

"Where are you from?" Egon asked more sternly.

"Egon. You're scaring her," Mags said.

Sierra's eyes raked the crowd. They were staring at her like she'd just grown a second head.

"Pardon my lack of manners my lady, but what she just did hasn't been seen since ancient times. Far more ancient than myself."

Mags tried to hide her surprise. She didn't know of anyone more ancient that Egon.

The sorcerer, Alissa entered the council chambers excitedly. "Master Egon. The spell worked. The darkness has vanished."

All eyes turned to Sierra in wonder and gratitude.

A blinding red light filled the throne room startling Ambro. He raced to the window overlooking the courtyard that reached from floor to ceiling and threw back the heavy red drapes covering the window.

He watched in a mixture of horror and amazement as the veil of darkness was lifted and replaced with pale sunlight. The light graced his hand. He didn't recoil from its warmth. It tingled his hand for a moment, then it was gone. Only the warmth remained.

He watched as long dead trees filled out with new leaves, and a long dried up river filled with water and fish. His mind raced. He knew that they would soon come for him.

He quickly crossed the room and banged the golden gong standing next to his throne. His dwindling army appeared, stunned and confused.

"The light has returned to our realm. It will not hurt us. It is time for the vampire nation to grow and prosper.

This is literally the dawn of a new day for our people. Go and explore this new land. Then return and let us plan for our future."

A cheer of excitement filled his throne room. He could play this new game, and he would play to win.

Dak felt Sierra shiver in fear. "Clear the room except for the council or I swear that I will take her away from here,' he cried out in anger.

Egon turned to the gallery, "Please do as he asked. All will be revealed in due time."

Dak escorted Sierra to an empty chair away from the council's wondering stare and took a seat next to her warning anyone foolish enough to approach.

"I apologize if in my excitement I frightened you," Egon stated. "My dear, we've never seen magic as powerful as the two of you combined that you demonstrated today. I've heard of such things, but it disappeared long ago."

Sierra stared at him in surprise. She didn't know what to say.

"Our magic has always been stronger when combined," Dak explained.

"How long have you possessed such powerful magic Dak?"

"I learned some magic while trapped in Bresslewood and Lady Mags has just started training me in the ways of magic."

Egon's head spun around and looked at Mags. "Is this true what he said?"

"Yes, why are you so surprised?"

"Only a select few of the vampires possess simple magic, but nothing like this," Egon exclaimed.

"Maybe because no one taught them how to use it," Mags defended.

"Light and dark have never been able to join their magic," he continued.

"Have the light and dark ever lived together and fallen in love?" she asked tiring of this silliness.

Sierra blushed to the roots of her hair.

Dak smiled and shrugged.

"It was long ago and they had to go through the transformation ritual."

Mags rolled her eyes. "And that was barbaric. As you can see, times have changed."

"Many things have changed while you were away. Much more than we could have predicted."

"This realm is no longer dark. Isn't that what you wanted? I don't understand what has you so concerned."

"There will be those who will fear or want to exploit their power," Egon said fearfully.

"You have experienced this yourself," Mags reminded him.

"I still bear those scars," Egon said softly.

"So do I," Mags said sadly. She had been led to believe that it was due to Egon's power that the lives of her family had been lost. But if Mavis was alive, could her parents still be alive?

Mags stood and crossed the room to stand next to Egon. She bent down next to him, taking his gnarled hand between hers. "If Mavis is alive they could be as well. I have to find her. I need this spell to protect myself and my people."

"Yes, of course." He glanced at Dak and Sierra. "You will keep them under your care?"

"I promise to guide them. They are fine young people. You have nothing to fear from them. Your land grows stronger. Together it will grow even stronger. We have one last piece of business to attend to after you teach me the spell," she smiled, squeezing Egon's hand affectionately.

"Business?"

"Ambro," she whispered.

"Ahh," he said smiling. He was going to enjoy a visit with Ambro.

The tension seemed to leave the room. Avis joined Dak and Sierra and introductions were made as Egon explained the binding blood spell to Mags.

A brief tour of the fortress was given before the council along with Mags, Sierra and Dak and Mags' army set off for Ambro's castle.

In just minutes, the land had come completely to life. Mountains had appeared out of nowhere, springs were fed by cascading waterfalls.

The forest was alive with animals and vegetation they had never seen before.

They arrived on the cobblestone street that led to the castle. The castle had been transformed. It sparkled gold in the sunlight. A fountain gurgled in the center of the courtyard.

Having heard their arrival, Ambro greeted them wearing a red and gold tunic. He opened his arms wide and said, "Welcome. Isn't it wonderful?"

He managed to shock them speechless. He spotted Dak in the crowd. "Dak, my boy. So good to see you. Please, everyone, come inside," he said, turning, giving them little choice except to follow.

"Is this a trick?" Sierra asked Dak, whispering softly to him.

"I wish I knew," he shrugged.

Ambro took his seat on his throne. "I accept whatever punishment you've come here to impose on me. What I did was terrible and I can only apologize for my misbegotten actions."

Egon eyed him with distrust. "Did you get hit on the head?" he asked, half serious.

Ambro laughed a deep rich laugh. "No. Something better. The light has cleared my dark soul. I feel like a new man."

"Could he be telling the truth?" Dak asked Mags.

"I guess it's possible."

Egon approached Mags. "Let the council meet with him to decide his fate. I mean no disrespect, but let's leave Sierra and Dak out of it. Their presence will only raise more questions."

"I agree."

"The council would like to meet with you in private." Egon said.

"Of course. We can meet in my chambers."

The six of them retreated to the King's chambers. Dak let out a sigh of relief. "I have no idea who that man is," he laughed.

"Maybe when the land was transformed, it transformed him as well," Sierra suggested.

"I hope so. So, what happened back there?"

"I have no idea, but I get the feeling that everyone is a little afraid of us."

"I get the same feeling and I don't like it," he said.

"Show me around your home. I want to see where you grew up."

"You do realize that it looks nothing like it did when I lived here?"

"I know, but I still want to see it."

Hand in hand Dak led her around the castle. They were both unaware that they were being watched as they moved through the castle.

Dak's once dark bedroom now had a light streaming through the window. He realized that this would never be his home again. His home would be wherever Sierra was. He smiled, pulling her into his arms, kissing her gently. "So," he said nervously. "Are we in love?"

Sierra blushed, kissing him. "I believe we are," she replied softly.

The council gathered on one side of the massive polished oak table, with Ambro sitting alone on the other side facing them with a smile planted on his weathered face.

"Don't fall for his games," Vestry said. "I doubt he's ever been sorry for a thing in his life."

Collin chuckled. "I have to agree with her."

Avis glared at Ambro, the man he'd once admired, looking for a crack in his armor of his newfound good humor. He couldn't tell if this was another of Ambro's games or if he had really been transformed with the realm.

"Where are our people that followed you here?" Avis asked concerned for their safety.

"I told them that they should explore this new land of ours and decide how we move forward from here," he answered honestly.

"How gracious from a man who is no longer their king," Vestry reminded him, her voice filled with disgust.

"True, I am no longer the king, but this is my land and they need to decide if they want to continue in my employment or venture out on their own."

"How's that?" Egon asked, in confusion.

"We have a realm to rebuild, not just the fortress you've built. A town to rebuild. To grow and prosper."

"That sounds all nice and good," Avis said. "How shall you be punished for starting a war?"

"If I can intercede on his behalf," Mags said. "There was some confusion on his part, spurred on by the fake giants. I think we should bind him to the land he professes to want to prosper and have the council monitor his actions. He is correct, that the realm needs to be rebuilt so it can grow and prosper."

Egon nodded in agreement. "That is a just idea."

"Agreed," Avis said.

Vestry and Collin nodded in agreement.

"If he starts anything we will lock him in the fortress dungeon," Collin added.

"All agree?" Egon asked.

"Aye," they answered together.

Egon cast a spell on Ambro and the land, binding the two together. "If you try to leave your land you will feel an intolerable pain."

"One word of advice, talk to your son before we leave," Avis said. You owe it to him and yourself."

"Thank you for your leniency." Ambro said. He already felt bound to his land and had no intention of leaving it.

Ambro bowed to them before leaving the room to search for his son.

"I don't trust him," Egon stated. "This was too easy."

"I'm sure we all agree on that," laughed Mags, following Egon from the room.

Ambro found Sierra and Dak in the courtyard, still unaware that they weren't alone. The spy was also unaware that he was being observed.

"Hello, young lady. I'm Ambro, Dak's father," he said joining them at the fountain, smiling warmly."

Taking his extended hand, she said, "Very nice to actually meet you."

"You lie charmingly well. I'm sure Dak's told you what a monster I am. But I promise, that is all behind me. The light has cured my dark heart and I ask for a chance to prove it to you."

Sierra extracted her hand from his. "I'll leave the two of you alone to talk."

Dak glared at her helplessly. He didn't want to be alone with his father.

Sierra shrugged and reentered the castle, joining the others in the main hall. She stood at the window so she could keep a watchful eye on Dak.

"I don't know where to start except to say that I'm sorry, and I love you," Ambro said, hugging Dak tightly.

Dak was stunned and returned the hug. This was a side of his father that he didn't know.

"I guess asking you to stay here is pointless. I saw the way you look at Sierra. She is lovely and charming. I am really happy for you."

"What was the council's decision?" Dak asked, uncomfortable discussing Sierra with him.

"I can't leave my land, or unbearable pain," he answered lightly.

"I hope you forget about war and make a fresh start."

"It would be easier with you by my side."

"I'm sorry. My place is with Sierra now."

"Be happy, my son, and please don't be a stranger."

Dak hugged Ambro again and together they walked back inside the castle. He hoped that his father had truly changed and regretted the things he had done.

Ambro served them refreshments and hugged Dak one last time before escorting them from the castle. He vowed to himself to make Dak proud of him again. He'd build up the vampire nation like nothing anyone had seen before.

In the courtyard, Dak turned and waved at his father.

Mags stopped at the fountain an unsettling feeling overcoming her. "Wait, I want to perform the blood binding spell now," she said urgently to Egon.

"Now, why now?"

"Something is happening. I can feel it," she whispered, fear threatening to overcome her.

"Come close everyone," Egon called out.

"Ashal norrid vestror elad." Mags whispered, cutting her hand with a small ivory handled knife. She moved through her people, touching each one of them with her bleeding hand.

The blood was quickly absorbed through their skin, protecting them from any spell Mavis would try to use against them.

She immediately felt better, but weak. "Thank you," she said to Egon.

"Safe trip home my lady," Egon said. Approaching Dak and Sierra, he said, "Take care of her."

"We will," they said in unison before climbing astride their horses. They bid the council farewell. Dak waved to his father one last time before they led their horses away from the castle.

Mags insisted that Sierra and Dak ride in the middle of her army for protection. Protection from what? She had no idea. She couldn't shake the uneasy feeling that something terrible was about to happen.

They entered the end of the Dark Realm, renamed the Awakening, by the council. It was simply breathtaking now that the darkness was gone.

They passed through the gate one by one, relieved to be returning home.

Sierra passed through behind Dak. He turned to say something and disappeared before her eyes.

Sierra screamed, calling his name.

Epilogue

Dak was thrown roughly to the ground in a dark, damp dungeon. He created a soft blue light so he could get a look around to try and determine where he was.

He could make out a set of stairs in front of his cell. He turned into a shadow and attempted to escape through the bars. To his surprise he couldn't pass through them.

Retaking his human form, he studied the bars closely. He knew a spell was preventing him from escaping. Did his father do this, he wondered.

He didn't have to wait long to find out. A slender figure was descending the stairs. Dak extinguished his light to wait.

A golden light appeared before him and a beautiful woman stood before him.

"I apologize if you were mistreated," she said. "You and I are going to become very good friends."

"I doubt that."

The woman's laughter filled the dark dank room.

The End

Secrets

Book Two - Eight Realm Series

Catherine Sitz

Chapter One

Dak

Dak studied the woman smiling at him from the other side of the bars. Something tugged at the back of his mind. She looked vaguely familiar.

"Now why don't you think we can be friends?" she asked.

"Oh, I don't know, maybe because I'm on this side of the bars, and I'm pretty sure that you put me here."

She smiled, her blue eyes twinkling. "You're only here for my protection."

Dak studied her closely. She had to be Mags' sister, Mavis. "Are you afraid of me?" he asked.

"Should I be?" she teased.

"So, where are we?"

"Somewhere safe," she smiled sweetly.

"I was safe before you snatched me," he reminded her.

Mavis frowned. "I like to think that I rescued you."

"From what?" he asked puzzled.

"Not what, whom," she answered cryptically. "Mags, of course."

"Of course," he repeated absently, wondering what her game was.

Mavis frowned angrily. "Are you mocking me?"

Dak smiled, showing off his pointed teeth as he leaned against the bars. "Now why would I do that? After all, we are such good friends, or we could be, if you would get me out of here."

"And then what?"

"We become friends," he said smiling.

"I think I feel safer with us becoming friends with you in there and me out here," she laughed.

"Well, I don't feel so safe being locked up in here. Is this really how you treat your friends?"

"I'm sorry you don't trust me, but you will. Please let me know what I can get you to make you more comfortable."

Dak turned and looked at the threadbare mattress and said, "I've got all the comforts of home. What could I possibly need?"

"You have a nasty streak," she said glaring at him with her hands on her slender hips.

"I do apologize. Being in a cage makes me a little testy."

"The sooner you behave yourself, the sooner you will be set free."

"And just what do I have to do to prove that I'm behaving?"

"No more smart remarks, would be a good start. I need you to trust me so I can show you the truth."

"What truth?"

"About Mags."

"What is the truth?"

"Did she tell you that she killed our parents and tried to kill me?" she said sadly.

Dak was stunned. Mags couldn't have hurt her family. He looked deep into Mavis' blue eyes. She either believed what she was saying or had told herself this lie so often, that she believed it.

He would have to play along or he'd never get out of the cell.

"You don't believe me?" she asked.

"I'm stunned. That's terrible. Why, why would she do something so horrible?"

"The kingdom of course."

"I'm sorry," he said sadly, pretending to go along with her.

Mavis' eyes opened wide with surprise. "What did you say?"

"I said, I'm sorry."

"You believe me?"

"I don't know what to believe, but I'm sorry that you lost your family."

Mavis studied Dak closely. Could he really believe her? She needed him to trust her, but this was entirely too easy. "You will be brought food and blankets. We will talk again tomorrow," she said, turning and disappearing back up the stairs.

Dak watched her go. He sat down on the cot, wondering how he was going to get out of this.

Mavis shut the door behind her and leaned against it. She had to make Mags pay for what she'd done.

Regaining her composure, she entered the large empty room. She never knew when they were watching her. She had to stay strong. She couldn't appear weak.

She could feel them around her, watching her every move. She wished they would show themselves.

One of the elders took form in front of Mavis, startling her. She stopped and studied the ethereal figure before her, masking her emotions.

They were a strange unfriendly race. No wonder the other realms knew very little about them.

"How is your prisoner?"

She wanted to scream at him that Dak was her guest, but conversation was a waste of time with them.

"He's fine," she replied, wishing he'd get on with the real reason he appeared before her.

"He will help you accomplish your task?"

"In time. I have to gain his trust first."

"His magic is strong enough?"

"I believe it is."

"Perfect. We are excited about this endeavor."

"I'm aware. But you must understand that it may take time to accomplish."

"We understand."

Mavis shivered. The way he spoke sounded like a threat. "Thank you," she said sweetly.

"I'll leave you to enjoy your evening," he said fading away.

Enjoy the evening, doing what? She left the castle and wondered around the palatial grounds before returning to the castle as darkness approached.

The palace was enormous and well kept. Framed pictures of landscapes dotted the marble walls. Mavis stopped in front of one that reminded her of home.

A pain of longing clutched her heart. She would make Mags pay for killing their parents. She wiped a single tear from her smooth cheek and continued exploring the castle.

She wondered outside to the balcony that overlooked the well-manicured lawn, framed by a dense forest. She wondered who kept everything in perfect order.

She couldn't imagine any of the invisibles that she'd met working in the yard or cleaning the palace. Were they able to maintain perfect order with magic? She had no idea how powerful they were, since they kept to themselves. Very little was known about them, except their current desire to increase the size of their realm.

She was afraid of what they would do to her if she failed. Shivering, she hugged herself and pushed the fear away.

Dak studied the sheet clad servants that brought him food and bedding. They were rail thin and extremely pail. They looked near death.

They floated more than they walked. He tried to get a look beneath their long flowing robes to see if they had feet.

Any attempt to engage them in conversation was ignored, so he watched them and learned. Odd, he couldn't tell if they were male or female.

They unlocked his cell and three of them entered. Two forced him into the corner, while the other one made up his bed.

"You could have just asked me to move," Dak said, staring at the two pale creatures in front of him.

One of them met his gaze with his dark empty eyes. "You are a prisoner. We don't make a point of conversing with prisoners," he said in a flat toneless voice that was dry and raw as if he spoke very little.

"And here I thought I was a guest," he laughed.

The invisible studied Dak, confused by his laughter. "You find it amusing being a prisoner?"

Dak smiled. "I find it amusing indeed."

The invisible was intrigued. He hadn't encountered anyone like Dak, not that he had encountered many outsiders.

The invisible making the bed finished and floated from the cell. The remaining two started backing slowly away from Dak.

"What's your name?" Dak asked, surprising him.

"Why do you ask?"

"It's customary to introduce oneself where I come from."

"I am called Falon," he said as he backed out of the cell, closing the door behind him.

"It's nice to meet you Falon," Dak said as the trio disappeared up the stairs leaving Dak alone, or so he hoped.

Well, that was weird, Dak thought to himself. He crossed the room, picked up his food tray off the table and sat down on the bed, studying the plate they'd prepared for him.

It looked like an assortment of meat and fruit he'd never seen before. He quickly ate and was surprised that it tasted better than it looked.

Finished, he floated the tray back to the table while casting a spell that would allow him to see the invisibles if they decided to spy on him. He was relieved to discover that he was alone.

He laid back against the soft pillows and decided to try and get some sleep.

He awoke the next morning to see Mavis studying him from the other side of the bars. An invisible was lurking in the corner unaware that Dak could see him.

"Good morning my lady," Dak said, sitting up, grinning at Mavis. "I'm hurt that you didn't tell our host that I'm a guest, not a prisoner."

Mavis glared at him, masking her frustration with his cavalier attitude. "Is everything a joke to you?" she asked.

Dak eased himself off the bed, slowly crossed the room, gripping the bars with both hands, he started at Mavis. "Why don't you stop playing games and tell me what you want from me."

This wasn't going at all how she'd planned. He wasn't afraid of her, and she wasn't certain she could control him. She exhaled softly. "I need your help," she said honestly.

"Asking would have worked much better than kidnapping me."

"I'm sure if I'd asked you to help me avenge my parent's death you'd have willingly agreed," she stated.

"Why do you think Mags is responsible?"

"That's what I was told. I was left for dead after we were attacked."

"Who told you this? Who found you?"

"Your father. He nursed me back to health and told me what my sister had done so she could control the realms."

Dak's eyes widened in surprise and anger. This explained so much. "I'm afraid you've been lied to," he said softly.

"You're calling your own father a liar?" she asked confused by his reaction.

"My father used you. He wanted to gain control of the eight realms."

Mavis turned away from Dak, her mind raced. This couldn't be true. She'd done terrible things to try to avenge the death of her parents. Mags had to be guilty. She turned back to face Dak. "This can't be true."

"Don't feel too bad. He lied to me too, for the same reason."

Mavis felt sick inside. "He betrayed his own son, but why?"

"Power. He's always envied the power you possessed."

"But you have the power of magic."

"Most of our magic is very limited."

"You are different, why?"

"I have no idea."

Dak glanced over at the invisible listening quietly in the corner. He had no reaction to their conversation.

Mavis was visibly struggling with what Dak had told her. "What do you need my help for?"

"The invisibles desire to increase the size of their realm."

Dak frowned, "Why?"

"I didn't ask. I agreed in return for their help."

"Their help to destroy Mags?"

Mavis lowered her head sadly, "Yes."

"I won't help you destroy Mags. I'm telling you the truth. She loved her parents. She loves you. She would never do anything to hurt anyone."

Tears streamed down Mavis' cheeks. "What have I done?" she cried in anguish, fleeing the room.

The invisible silently followed her.

Mavis raced from the room, up the wide marble staircase to her room at the top of the stairs. She threw herself across the enormous four poster bed and cried silently into the pillows.

Four invisibles watched her silently with interest.

www.ingramcontent.com/pod-product-compliance
Lightning Source LLC
Chambersburg PA
CBHW070833020826
48982CB00019B/1088/J